SURVIVORS

FLOOD
MISSISSIPPI, 1927

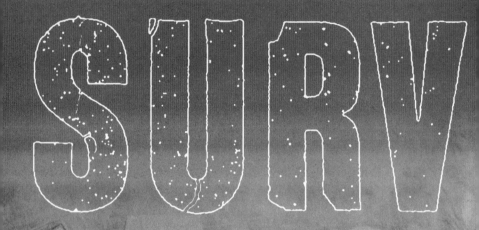

SURV

Don't miss any of these survival stories:

TITANIC

FIRE

EARTHQUAKE

BLIZZARD

And coming soon:

DEATH VALLEY

VORS

FLOOD
MISSISSIPPI, 1927

KATHLEEN DUEY
and KAREN A. BALE

Aladdin

New York   London   Toronto   Sydney   New Delhi

ALADDIN

An imprint of Simon & Schuster Children's Publishing Division

1230 Avenue of the Americas, New York, NY 10020

This Aladdin hardcover edition March 2015

Text copyright © 1998 by Kathleen Duey and Karen A. Bale

Jacket illustration copyright © 2015 by David Palumbo

Also available in an Aladdin paperback edition.

For information about special discounts for bulk purchases, please contact Simon & Schuster

Special Sales at 1-866-506-1949 or business@simonandschuster.com.

The Simon & Schuster Speakers Bureau can bring authors to your live

event. For more information or to book an event contact the Simon & Schuster

Speakers Bureau at 1-866-248-3049 or visit our website at www.simonspeakers.com.

Jacket design by Jeanine Henderson

Interior designed by Tom Daly

The text of this book was set in Berling LT Std.

Manufactured in the United States of America 0215 FFG

2 4 6 8 10 9 7 5 3 1

Library of Congress Control Number 98-19349

ISBN 978-1-4814-1643-6 (hc)

ISBN 978-1-4814-1642-9 (pbk)

ISBN 978-1-4814-1644-3 (eBook)

For the women who taught us the meaning of courage:
Erma L. Kosanovich
Katherine B. Bale
Mary E. Peery

Chapter One

Molly Bride could hear the river. It sounded like a hard wind. The rain had started again, and her faded yellow shift was wet through, plastered across her back. The path was underwater from the mule shed on. Feeling something sharp stab at her heel, she took an uneven step to the side, splashing brown water on her hem. She balanced herself, reaching out to grip the rain-slick fence rail. She pulled her foot out of the sucking mud, twisting around to look. No blood.

Molly started up the path again, walking more slowly, swatting at the mosquitoes that whined close to her ears. Her family had owned this farm for ten years, and they were still picking up broken glass. The Porter boys had used this end of the farmyard for target practice. They must have shot up a thousand soda pop bottles, learning to aim straight. She sighed and glanced upward, squinting against the rain. Was it ever going to stop?

The wind drove the spattering raindrops against the side of the chicken coop as Molly swung the door open and stepped over the threshold. She was greeted with startled clucking from the rows of low roosts. Pa's favorite speckled Dominique hen darted out of the shadows, and Molly dodged her pecking beak, then bent to pin her wings and lift her to eye level. "You ought to know better than to try that with me," she scolded.

The hen struggled, and Molly set her atop the nest shelf and backed up quickly. The floor planks were slippery. The standing water was seeping up from below the floor.

Molly shook her finger at the speckled hen. "You just stay put, now." She glanced away, then back when she saw the hen spread her wings a little. "I said stay put! You peck me even once, and I'll throw you out into that storm, and you won't get warm for a week."

The hen made a resentful grinding sound and settled, lowering her wings and flattening her feathers. Only then did Romeo, the brown-and-white rooster, come out from under the old corncrib built along the far wall. He approached slowly, marching proudly, his arched tail swinging from side to side.

"You'll have to wait for Meachum to bring you supper scraps," Molly told him. "Mama just sent me out for eggs."

Just as she finished speaking, the wind shoved against the coop again, and Molly felt the planks shudder beneath her feet. The whole shed rocked and trembled. A chorus of squawking rose from the frightened hens. "No wonder you aren't laying," Molly murmured as she checked the nests.

She found four eggs in the damp straw. Only four. That would barely be enough for this morning's griddle cakes. Her mother was going to be upset—and the tawny hen was still missing. Maybe a fox had gotten her. Or she was setting somewhere under the mule shed or the porch, trying to hatch a clutch of eggs.

Molly's mother had been pretty testy lately. The rain was on everyone's nerves. Every time they took the truck into town, the water seemed higher. Driving along the top of the levee was strange now. Usually, the river wasn't anywhere close. You couldn't even see it through the stands of willow and pine and the tangle of weeds and tye vines that grew along its banks.

Now, the dark brown water had covered all that and come up over the cleared berm. The deep barrow pit at the toe of the levee had filled up weeks ago. Then the water had risen up the slope. The past few days the river had been lapping at the levee road.

Molly gathered her hem in one hand, placing the eggs into the folds of the soft cotton. Careful not to bump them against the coop door, she went out. The wind chilled her and she shivered, stepping back into the cold mud.

Molly glanced across the yard, beyond the outhouse, at the slope that led up to the road. A steamboat had gone past yesterday, hugging the levee for some reason. She had craned her neck to watch it go by, so far above her that it was like looking up at the second story of the jailhouse. If the levee ever broke here, the river would come crashing through the crevasse. . . . She shook her head and forced the thought away.

Molly started for the house, walking slowly, feeling her way up the submerged path. Backwater was widening the bayou and muddying the canebrakes on the far side of the north pasture. She could see the lightning tree from here—or at least the stark, barkless top of it. Garrett had said to meet him there as early as she could this evening so they could work on their raft.

Molly picked her way past the mule shed. It was going to be hard to sneak off. Both her brothers were keeping close to home now, and neither one of them liked her being friends with a white boy. They would have been furious if they had known the whole truth.

She and Garrett were partners. Hidden high in the lightning tree, they had an old molasses jar half full of pennies and nickels and dimes. They were saving up from Garrett's odd jobs and her sewing and cleaning for Mrs. Spiars at the boardinghouse in Mayersville. Someday, they both wanted to see places like London or Paris, or at least Vicksburg.

The wind gusted, and the cold rain stung Molly's cheeks. Just then, Meachum came into sight, walking back along the levee road, hunched against the wind. Bedraggled, Skipper trotted close at his heels, his ears and tail low.

Meachum had been working for Mr. Turner, sandbagging the edge of the bayou to keep the old man's fields from filling up with backwater. Lawrence had been working for Turner, too, until Pa had made him quit. There was too much to do around home now to spare both boys.

Meachum's lowered head and slogging pace told Molly he was tired. Since he had turned thirteen and started hiring out, he wasn't nearly as mischievous as he had been a year before. Lawrence, at sixteen, liked to play at being a man. He was starting to order her and Meachum around when Pa wasn't looking. Though Molly loved her brothers, she sometimes wished for a sister to share chores and secrets with— but Hope was still just a baby.

"Molly!"

She looked up, blinking, to see through the rain. Her father was standing on the porch, his hands on his hips. "We were beginning to think you got lost!"

Molly grinned at the teasing in his voice. She heard him laugh before he turned to go back in. She hurried as fast as she dared through the deep puddles below the pigsty and the cowshed. When the path veered up toward the house, she walked faster, mud oozing up between her bare toes.

Meachum made it inside just before she did. As

Molly opened the door, she saw him pulling off his wet shirt, hanging it on the clothes wire above the cookstove. Pa was standing close to Hope's cradle, rocking it gently. Ma had the kerosene lantern hung above the sink. She was adding last night's coffee grounds to the scrap bucket. The cast-iron pot was already on the stove, steaming. Molly could smell the warm odor of grits cooking. Her mouth watered.

Meachum opened the fire door and shoved in a piece of split oak. "The bayou up along Turner's place is all right."

Molly saw her father nod. "Sandbags holding?"

Meachum shrugged. "For now. Lawrence went upriver a little to get a look at the levee. There's a crew from the Corps up there—"

"Put your trust in the Army Corps of Engineers!" Pa interjected. "I will tell you one thing. The day those ol' boys tell me to evacuate, I'm going to laugh in their faces. Back in twenty-two they proved one thing to me. It's in God's hands, not theirs."

Molly kept quiet as a mouse in a corncrib. The last thing she wanted to do was get her father going about Major Donald Connolly and all the rest of the bigwigs and their predictions.

"You have the eggs, Molly?"

Startled by the harshness in her mother's voice, Molly turned. "Only four," she said, spilling them gently onto her cot.

Her mother frowned and said nothing more as she scooped up the eggs. Molly glanced away. There was nothing to do but wish the rain would stop, and she was already doing that a dozen times a day. Everyone was. Wishing and praying, but none of it was doing any good.

Molly waited for Meachum to step away from the stove before she walked into the little kitchen. Turning her back, she shimmied off her wet shift and took down her dry one. Shivering in her damp slip, she pulled it over her head, then stood close to the stove. This was last year's dress and it was too tight across her shoulders.

Molly leaned close to the stove, letting the waves of heat soak into her skin. Her mother handed her a wooden spoon and slid the big pot toward her. "The grits are thickening. Don't you let them scorch."

Molly started stirring, wincing when the bubbles burst and the hot grits spattered her wrists. After a few minutes, she pulled the pot aside, sliding it across the stove top, away from the firebox. The bubbles slowed.

The door suddenly banged open. A gust of wet wind came in as Lawrence stumbled over the threshold. "The levee," he managed between breaths. "There's a little water coming over the top, Pa!"

Molly watched her father run out the door. An instant later, both her brothers followed him, carrying empty feed sacks and shovels and splashing their way toward the river. Her mother was crying.

Chapter Two

"Hey, Mr. Talbot." Garrett Wood pulled off his cap and stood in the doorway of Whittacher's Grocery. The water in the street had gotten deep enough to cover the top step. Little rivulets were flowing inside and puddling near the threshold. Garrett stared at his bare feet. They weren't too muddy. He stood on one foot and rubbed the other against the back of his pant leg, then switched.

"Is that you, Garrett?" Old Man Talbot was stacking cans on a shelf behind the counter. He did not turn around. The lights flickered, and Garrett heard the Delco plant that sat out beside the store on a cement slab run rough for a second. Then the motor caught up again.

"Mama sent me after chickpeas and ten pounds of flour," Garrett said a little louder. He waited, fiddling with his burlap sack. He looked from the bolts of brightly colored cloth to the fragrant Florida oranges in the crates stacked by the door. There were pairs of leather shoes hanging from a wire strung over the counter. He stared at them with genuine longing, then looked back down at his feet. Little cuts crisscrossed his skin, and one of his toenails was black from stubbing. He cleared his throat politely.

Mr. Talbot finally faced him. "I'll get them for you, but you tell your mama that she had best come see Mr. Whittacher about her account."

"Yes sir, I'll tell her." Garrett said it quickly, and glanced back outside. Willard and Earle Harland were waiting for him across the street. Willard was throwing pebbles into the muddy stream of water that had appeared two weeks ago behind the courthouse. It was twice as wide as it had been a few days before.

"Hurry up, Garrett," Earle shouted.

Garrett pretended he hadn't heard. Mr. Talbot laid the flour on the counter. The cloth sack was blue with green stripes. Mr. Talbot bent down, then straightened again, placing a pile of eight or ten empty flour sacks on the counter. "You can take these, too. I had to spill them out. The flour got wet and rotted."

Garrett hid a smile. Mr. Talbot knew that the colored flour sacks meant a lot to Mama, because she used them to make dresses for the girls. Ivy and Mae were barely four and would be delighted at the gift. Ginny, at nine, was beginning to wish for store-bought clothes.

Garrett tightened his hands into fists for an instant. He was going to find a good job in Greenville, or Rolling Fork, or Yazoo City, or somewhere, and he was going to make it so that Mama would never have to worry about money again. As he always did, he felt guilty for a few seconds about the money he and Molly had hidden up the lightning tree. Then he promised himself for the hundredth time that he wouldn't squander a penny. He would use it to make that good job possible.

"Come on, Garrett!"

This time it was Willard. Mr. Talbot was scooping the chickpeas into a paper bag. He rolled the top shut and tied the parcel with twine. Garrett put the groceries into his sack. Then he nodded and smiled his way out the door, plopping his cap back on his head. He slung the sack over his shoulder and waded back into the brownish water. He winced, sloshing across the patch of sharp red gravel that Whittacher's spread in front to keep down the mud. He shook his head. It sure wasn't doing the job this year.

"Let's go see the cottonmouth they killed out at the Indian mound," Willard said as Garrett got closer. "Earle saw it, didn't you, Earle?"

"Sure did." Earle slapped a mosquito on his arm. "It was lying on a tombstone up there, one of the old Heath-Smith graves. They hung it on the fence. Biggest moccasin I ever saw."

Garrett hesitated. He wouldn't mind seeing the snake, but he didn't want to go with Willard and Earle. Lately all Earle thought about was smoking cigarettes and flirting with girls—and Willard was just plain mean-hearted. "I suppose I had better just get on home," he said evenly.

"Why? You afraid of snakes?" Willard threw another rock. The muddy water splashed up in a little plume.

Garrett shook his head, refusing to rise to the bait.

Willard grimaced. "I know," he said slowly. "You have to get home so you can go meet up with that darky gal, don't you? She's just your best friend, isn't—"

"I told you to leave off about Molly," Garrett cut in.

Willard lowered his voice. "You know what folks say about you?"

Garrett hitched the sack higher on his shoulder and started walking. There was no point in arguing with the Harland brothers. His daddy had always said that some folks would live and die ignorant, no matter what. Garrett felt the stab of sadness that thoughts about his father always brought.

As he continued on down Court Street toward the levee, a truck horn blared. Garrett saw Mr. Wade's truck rolling toward him, sending up sprays of water from either side of the tires.

"Go on, then," Willard was shouting. "We didn't want you to come, anyway. We was just being polite."

Garrett half-turned and touched his cap in a mock salute. Then he quickened his pace, making his way around a deep puddle at the toe of the levee. He started up the slope, following the path. Halfway up the levee he turned and looked back down Court Street. The tin roof of the courthouse matched the gray sky. Beyond it, people's houses stood along a graveled road that ran east between muddy, unplowed cotton fields.

The smell of frying bacon tickled at Garrett's nose, and he wished he had money for a restaurant meal. Sighing, he went on up the slope of the levee, nodding politely at four men who were unloading sandbags.

There were a number of trucks and cars up on the levee. Convicts in striped uniforms went past him heading north, carrying shovels, their legs chained together. Farther along, a crew of colored workmen were laying down sandbags.

Garrett was glad he hadn't gone with Willard and Earle. He had to stop off at old Miss Hampstead's place and carry in her wood. Then, he had to finish tearing the tye vine off the cowshed and muck out the chicken coop before he went to meet Molly— and he wanted to clean up the length of rope he'd found. He walked faster, shivering as it began to rain hard again.

Chapter Three

Molly straightened up, glancing uneasily at the river. It seemed to stretch all the way to forever. She wondered if the people on the Arkansas side of the river were as worried as everyone in Mississippi. Her father and Lawrence were positioning the last two bags. Breathing hard, Meachum stood to one side. The low spot in the levee was repaired now, the new sandbags holding the pressure of the water. It had taken hours. Molly had brought noontime biscuits and pie, then stayed on to help.

The rain picked up a little. Molly saw her father shake his fist at the sky. "We'll never make a cotton crop if this won't let up," he shouted.

Lawrence scuffed his foot across the sandbags.

"Charley says his pa is going to plant corn next week no matter what."

"He's a fool if he does," Pa snapped. "The seed will just rot." He hitched up his overalls. "We're going to walk along the levee, see if Mrs. Wood needs any help. Molly, you go tell your ma that everything is all right now."

Molly stared at the new sandbags. They were already turning dark, the color of the roiling water.

"Molly! You hear me?"

"Yes, Pa," she answered. Her father made a shooing motion. She turned and made her way back along the levee. There was a nearly constant stream of trucks now. It seemed like everybody and his brother were trying to keep the river from flooding.

She was chilled so she ran down the long incline of the levee to warm up, then kept running, startling the mules when she splashed past their corral.

"Everything is all right," Molly said as she opened the door—before her mother could notice Pa and the boys weren't with her. Then she explained where they had gone.

Her mother lifted her hands toward heaven. "That levee scares me to death." She straightened her apron. "Hope is napping, so maybe we could get started shelling butter beans. One of these days that upper garden has to dry out enough to plant."

Molly nodded. Pa had built shelves along the rear wall of their little parlor. He was smart, Molly thought, as she pushed aside the pink draperies Ma had made to cover the containers of seed. The mice and mildew in the barn were bad any year. This year, the moisture would have ruined all the seed.

The butter bean hulls rustled in the half-bushel basket as Molly carried it out to the worktable in the kitchen. Her mother was wiping the table clean with a dishcloth.

"I wonder if we will get enough of a crop to be able to put up any beans this year." She sighed. "The home demonstration agent that was up in Rolling Fork last month told Hannah Franklin that it isn't safe to can beans without a pressure cooker."

Molly looked out the window. The rain was letting up.

"Those ladies say a lot of things that would sure surprise the old-timers. My mother put up beans every year. No one ever got sick that I can recall."

Molly nodded, her hands automatically beginning

to work. She pinched the brittle hulls just hard enough to pop them open. Then she ran her thumb down the inside curve of the pod, first one side, then the other. The beans rattled into the clean bowl her mother had brought. Molly deftly flipped the empty hulls to the other end of the table.

"The cistern is full. I dragged the cover back over it. The water looks a little cloudy. I am going to start boiling it. Vera May says the telephone operators down in Vicksburg are telling everyone who places a call to boil their water for twenty minutes. She says they're afraid of epidemics."

Molly half-listened. Her mother was lonely, she knew. They hadn't been to church in three weeks. The building stood in a low spot; it was flooded up to the choir loft.

Molly's hands went about their work as her thoughts strayed to Garrett and their new raft. Last year's rope had come from a washed-up crate they had found and it had rotted. Garrett thought he'd seen some in a shed at his place. She just hoped there was enough.

"You're sure not talkative today," Molly heard her

mother say once the bowl was nearly full of beans for the third time.

"I'm sorry." Molly stood to clear off the dry hulls, dumping them into the kindling box. She looked sidelong at her mother. "I guess I'll go on out if you don't need more help." Molly saw a frown cross her mother's face, and she felt a little guilty.

"I know what you're up to," her mother said.

Molly ducked her head.

"Your father and I just don't want your feelings hurt, Molly. In a year or two that boy is going to have his own friends."

Molly refused to answer. They had had this talk before. "You be home well before dark, young lady," her mother said. "That gives you less than an hour."

Molly knew Ma liked Garrett. He was always polite and respectful, and he kept his fingernails clean, like a storekeeper. If she *hadn't* liked him, it wouldn't matter what color his skin was, she'd have kept Molly home.

"If you're going, you'd better hurry."

"I'll be quick as I can," Molly said. She kissed her mother on the cheek, then went out.

◊ ◊ ◊

Garrett ended up shoveling mud out of Miss Hampstead's cow barn, then carrying in her wood for the week. Once he was home, he went straight to the far pasture and spent two hours ripping the tye vine off the shed. It had grown into the crevices between the planks and had mounded up around the piling timbers.

Then, hungry, but not wanting to stop to eat, he started in on the chicken coop. Once he had finished that nasty job, he washed up at the pump, dousing his head and hair, trading a wet shirt on the clothesline for the one he had on.

It was raining hard again as he threw his dirty shirt into the laundry tub and started for the porch. He pushed the dogs aside with his knees, holding the flour sacks above his head as he squeezed in the front door and set down his sack. His mother's face lit up with a wide smile. "Mr. Talbot is one thoughtful gentleman, isn't he? Girls? Girls, come look."

Garrett stood back as his sisters' bedroom door banged open and they spilled out. Ginny was first, her pretty face somber as always. The twins were giggling, chasing each other. Ivy bumped into Mae, sending her careening into the sideboard. Before

Mae could start crying, Garrett's mother swooped her up, distracting her with kisses and a bright smile.

"Look at all these! There's red for Ginny and—"

"Blue for us!" Mae shouted.

Ivy began repeating it in a singsong rhythm. "Blue for us, blue for us, blue for us . . ."

Garrett's mother smiled, but he could see circles beneath her eyes, and he was suddenly aware of the mended holes in her apron.

"Tomorrow, I'll see if I can bring home a rabbit or a squirrel," he said.

His mother looked at him over Mae's soft curls. "Rabbit stew would be a treat. I hate to kill any more of the hens—we have fewer and fewer eggs to sell in town as it is. I can't expect Mr. Talbot to keep extending us credit when we don't even have cotton planted."

"No one does, Mama," Garrett said, then pressed his lips together. He would put off saying anything about needing to settle their account as long as he could.

Usually, by this time of year, he had the vegetable garden in and the east field plowed for corn and cotton. Money was going to be scarcer than ever this year. Maybe Mr. Talbot would let him work off the amount they owed by helping at the store. Garrett chided himself. He would have thought to ask if the danged Harlands hadn't been there, bothering him.

"Mrs. Todd was saying today that she was going to her sister's in Vicksburg if the river doesn't go down soon," Garrett's mother said.

"Molly's pa says he won't leave no matter what."

Garrett's mother frowned. "With all due respect for Joseph Bride's opinions, I have decided to take you and the girls to Yazoo City. We can stay with my aunt Julia Pearl."

Garrett stared at her. "When? You mean if the levee breaks up at Leota or—"

"I just don't know. Maybe it'd be foolish to wait that long."

Garrett studied her face. She was still undecided, he was sure. And sometimes it took Mama weeks to decide things. "I'm going to go down by the bayou," Garrett said evenly, hoping his mother would be too preoccupied to ask him more. She smiled, then waved one hand at him as Mae and Ivy began dividing the flour sacks into two piles, playing dress shop.

Garrett went outside. The clouds were still dark

and low, but the rain had stopped, at least for now. He pulled the rope out of the shed where he had found it and tied it between the clothesline posts. He wet burlap feed sacks at the hand pump and used them to rub it up and down, scrubbing off four years' worth of mouse droppings and farm dust. The fiber was still sound and strong. When the rope was clean, he coiled it and set off toward the bayou, scolding the dogs to make them stay.

The rain had started up again as he walked the turnrow closest to the levee. He pulled his cap lower and shrugged his shirt higher on his neck. It wasn't really cold, but he was sick of being chilly. It seemed like forever since the sun had been out long enough to really warm him through.

The water came up over the turnrow above the west field. Garrett set down the coil of rope to roll his pant legs up a little higher, then went on. Like he always did, he avoided looking at the unplowed ground. This field had lain fallow since his daddy had died. Maybe this spring he'd be able to bring himself to go into it.

Garrett blinked, fighting a sudden memory of his father's twisted form between the seed rows. Heart failure, the doctor had said. Garrett pushed his hair out of his face, remembering how hot it had been that day, how Jake had stood still in the harness for hours to avoid trampling his father's body. Jake was the best red mule in the county.

Garrett wiped at his eyes, then smiled a little. That was one good thing about this rain. No one could tell he'd been crying.

He skirted along the edge of the woods, careful to keep his eyes on the path ahead. Crossing the slippery log bridge that spanned the narrowest part of the bayou, the water was so high that when he jumped off the end of the bridge, he splashed in almost up to his knees. He waded out, shifting the heavy rope from his right shoulder to his left.

Once he was back among the trees, Garrett tried to hurry, watching the grassy ground. A movement in the grass made him pause mid-step and he stumbled, lurching to one side. A second later, there was a tiny rustle behind him, a sound so small that he wasn't sure he had even heard it above the rain. But he whirled around, his heart thudding in his chest. He stared at the grass.

After a few seconds, Garrett turned again,

scanning the ground closest to his feet. Then, turning once more, he let his eyes search a larger circle. A whispering sound off to his right brought him wheeling around once more. The rope banged against his shoulder as he stood nervously. He couldn't see anything.

Rattlesnakes were usually shy and would get out of the way if given a chance. But if it was a copperhead or a water moccasin . . . He had killed four this spring, and every time he had been uneasy for an hour afterward. They were bad this year. Mama had gotten so she wouldn't let the girls stray out of the home yard. Inside the fence, the dogs and chickens would set up a warning ruckus if they saw a snake.

Cautiously, Garrett took a step, then another. Then, when a hissing sound erupted behind him, he very nearly jumped out of his skin. He whirled, positive that he was about to see a snake in the grass, chasing him. Instead, he saw nothing. Then he heard the giggling.

"You look awful scared, Garrett Wood."

It took him a second to spot Molly. She had climbed a chinaberry tree. She dropped a handful of pebbles and twigs, then slid down, grinning at him.

"If I was you, Molly Bride, I'd run."

She only put her hands on her hips. "Well then, good thing you're not me. Because I am way too smart to be running through these ol' woods barefoot in the rain. There could be snakes."

Garrett tried to keep his face rigid, frowning, but he could feel the corners of his mouth tugging upward. Molly's grin widened. She rounded her eyes and mimicked him, turning in a slow circle, staring wildly at the grass.

"Come on, you fool," he said, to keep himself from laughing aloud.

"The bayou is backing up," Molly said as she turned and led the way into the woods. She angled onto the game trail that led to their clearing. The path was narrow, worn by possums and raccoons and deer.

When they climbed the levee to skirt a patch of poison oak, he could see that the sun was going down somewhere behind the blanket of clouds. The water was getting darker, along with the sky. He couldn't see the Arkansas shore.

Ahead of him, Molly was walking slowly, staring at the foamy water that lapped along the edge of the levee. He looked back down into the treetops. The

bayou was filling up from all the rain. A few weeks
before, it had been about half as wide.

Garrett slid the rope from his shoulder as they
came off the levee. An armadillo scuttled into the
brush as he followed Molly along the edge of the
bayou where their lightning tree stood on its weed-
choked island. In the dusky light Garrett could see
the raft. It was aground, lying slantwise above the
bayou where they had left it in December when cold
weather set in.

"Oh, my Lord," Molly said abruptly. She pointed.

Garrett followed her gesture. The narrow island
that had stood in the middle of the bayou all his life
had disappeared beneath the rising backwater. There
was a decided slant to their lightning tree. Maybe the
water was undermining its roots. Maybe they had
rotted, and the tree was finally going to fall.

"Our money," Molly breathed.

Garrett clenched his fists and nodded. "We should
have thought of this," he said. "I never imagined the
backwater would get this high."

Molly was shaking her head, and he knew she was
trying not to cry. "It took us three years to save it up,"
she whispered after a few seconds.

"It'll be all right," Garrett said, not believing it but praying that it was true. "We'll fix the raft."

"Come on," Molly said, tugging at his sleeve.

Garrett started toward the raft, uncoiling the rope as he went. "Help me."

Molly hesitated only a second, then followed, dropping to her knees beside the raft. "You pull, I'll knot—I'm faster."

Garrett nodded. He used his pocketknife to cut the frayed rope free of the logs. Molly dragged each one clear, lining them up again. Garrett kept glancing at the darkening sky.

Garrett doubled the rope, fitting the looped end around the first log. Then he crossed the ends of the rope and stood aside while Molly tied the knot. When she moved, he lifted the next log to pass one of the ropes beneath it, pulling the long ends through. Molly tied the second knot as he held the logs tightly.

At the end of the first row of knots, Garrett rocked back on his heels and drew the ropes across the face of the end log. Molly tied a lark's head to reverse the direction of the rope. Then they set to work again.

Garrett tried to hurry. Molly tied the knots as fast

as she could each time, then got out of his way while he hauled the rope between the next two logs. The rope sang against the wood as Garrett jerked it into place. Without speaking, they finished the second row and reversed the rope once more.

"It's getting too dark," Molly said between her teeth as they worked. "Ma will worry if I'm gone much longer."

Garrett glanced up at the sky, then sidelong at the bayou. The water looked like ink. He kept working doggedly, furious with himself for not checking their lightning tree sooner.

"We can't go out there now," Molly said as they finished the last row of knots.

Garrett stood up and realized he could barely see her face. "I have to work for Mr. Lawlor all day tomorrow and most of Wednesday."

Molly bent to break off a piece of grass, then stood silently, staring out across the bayou. "Don't you try it alone," Garrett said. "Promise me."

Molly didn't answer immediately. She sighed first. "All right. I'll wait for you. Wednesday afternoon, then?"

He nodded, unable to stop staring at the ghostly

shape of the lightning tree against the darkening sky. "We best get home. Walk the levee. Snakes aren't as likely up there."

"'Night," Molly said, then turned and ran toward the levee road.

The rain began to fall harder, and a sigh of wind chilled Garrett. The roaring of the river seemed louder for an instant, and he shook his head. Without looking back at the leaning tree that held three years' hard work and most of his dreams, he started home.

Chapter Four

Wednesday, Molly got up early. With half her mind worrying about the lightning tree, she fed the chickens, set out the lettuce plants her mother had started in the cold frame, fed the pigs, and cleaned off the old bean stalks from the picket fence. The garden was soppy. When she dug the little holes for the lettuce plants, they seeped half full of water. Her mother was going to be upset if they just rotted in the ground, but Molly was pretty sure that was what was going to happen.

Meachum and Lawrence and her father spent the early afternoon walking the levee again. By late afternoon, Molly was watching for a chance to slip away. Her mother kept glancing at her.

"Molly, you are acting like a nervous colt. What in

the world is the matter? Is the rain on your nerves, too?"

Molly shrugged. She and Garrett had made a pact; they would never tell anyone else about the money jar. Ever. She tried not to look out the little kitchen window. It would do no good. The lightning tree had either fallen, or it hadn't. No amount of stewing would make a difference.

"What is on your mind, child?"

Molly looked up at her mother. She was mending. Hope was at her feet, playing with a basket full of empty thread spools, clacking the wood together and murmuring quietly to herself.

"I am so tired of rain," Molly said softly.

Her mother set her mending aside and stood up, her stockinged feet silent on the linoleum. She put her arms around Molly and hugged her hard for a few seconds. "Would you go cut some cane for garden stakes? I want to tie up the sweet peas this year, see if we can't keep the beetles out of them. And you can keep an eye out for that tawny hen."

Molly stood up so quickly that she saw a look of surprise cross her mother's face. She half-turned to avoid her mother's studying eyes.

"Take the hand ax for the cane," her mother said. "And some twine to tie up the bundles."

Molly went into the kitchen and pulled open the bottom drawer of the Hoosier cabinet. The hand ax lay on top of the garden trowels and Papa's tin snips. She pulled it out, then straightened up and got the garden knife from the sideboard. Mama reached up to take the ball of twine down from its shelf and wound a length of it around her fingers. Molly fished a salt sack out of the bin and put the ax in it.

"Be careful," her mother said, holding out the twine between her hands. Molly cut it, then put the ball her mother had wound into the sack along with the knife. "Watch where you're walking, and not just for snakes," her mother was saying. "Did I tell you that Dudley Stanton saw a bobcat less than a stone's throw from their porch in the middle of the day?"

"I'm always careful," Molly told her.

Hope was trying to stand. Molly's mother reached down to help her, looking up just once as Molly went out the door. "You be back before dark."

"I will," Molly promised, then turned and skipped down the steps, slinging the sack over her shoulder. She waded through the worst of the water in the yard, then crossed behind the chicken coop, following the path along the edge of the big field. There, in the distance, she could see the top of the lightning tree. It was still slanted, but it hadn't fallen yet. Once she knew her mother couldn't see her, she started to run.

The tallest stand of cane was just east of the old log bridge. She whistled twice. When Garrett didn't answer, she chopped one stout piece of cane and used it to beat noisily against the stand. She kept up the clatter long enough to scare any snake into showing itself. Then, she set to work. She chopped stalk after stalk with the hand ax, then, careful of the razor-sharp edges where the cane had shattered, she trimmed the narrow, stiff leaves near the top. As she knotted the twine around two good-sized bundles, she kept glancing off toward the bridge.

The afternoon cool had settled in. It'd be dusky before too much longer. Where was Garrett? She put everything back in the sack, then shouldered it, wishing she hadn't promised him she wouldn't try alone. What if he couldn't come? Just then, she heard his high-pitched whistle and ran to meet him as he crossed the bridge. "Did you see it? It's still standing!"

Garrett came across before he answered. His cheeks were flushed, and he was breathing hard. "I came down to check on my way home from Mr. Lawlor's," he told her without breaking stride. "The water is a lot higher than when we were here last, Molly."

Molly shrugged. "If we don't get our money now, Garrett, we may never." She glanced back at the bundles of cane. "Mama sent me to cut garden stakes."

"Let's carry them with us. I'll help you get them home once we've gotten the jar."

Molly led the way. The cane was heavy and awkward, and they had to walk slowly through the woods.

Molly dumped her bundle near the raft and dropped the sack beside it. "I've got a hand ax, some twine, and a knife in there, if that helps us any."

Garrett let his cane bundle slide to the ground. "Might. Bring the sack, anyway."

Molly nodded, staring at the high water. "Did you see if the poles are still where we left them?"

Garrett nodded. "I'll get them."

Molly watched him sprint toward a big willow

tree and disappear under its drooping branches. A moment later, he emerged, carrying both poles. His was longer and a little heavier. They had spent hours scrubbing them with sand to smooth the wood.

"Ready?" Garrett nodded at her. They laid their poles across the logs. Then, Molly helped him drag the raft into the shallows. The bottom was muddy. Once they were wading in water up to their knees, Molly slung her sack onto the raft. She turned to sit down on the logs, swinging her legs around quickly before the raft had time to tilt. As Garrett got on, she leaned to balance his weight. She picked up her pole and held it ready, waiting.

Together they pushed off, guiding the raft out onto the dark water. The pole felt familiar in Molly's hands—rafting reminded her of summer, of days so hot the bayou water was warm to the touch.

Guiding the raft carefully, they worked together to position it as close to the trunk of the lightning tree as they could. Once it was alongside, Garrett jabbed his pole into the mud, angling it against the raft to hold it steady. "You brace from that side," he said.

Molly nodded, sinking the end of her pole in the mud as he had done, but keeping hold of it. She watched as he stood, cautiously straightening up until he was sure of his balance. Then he leaned out and grasped a low branch of the lightning tree. He scrambled upward, quick and agile, and Molly allowed herself a smile. In a moment, they would have their money and all they would have to do would be to figure out another hiding place for the jar. It was getting dark fast, and Molly glanced up at the sky. Clouds were closing in, thickening; nightfall would come early.

A loud, cracking sound startled her out of her thoughts. Garrett was halfway up now, clinging to the trunk where it tapered into a slender column. "It's falling!" he shouted. The tree slowly sagged away from Molly, then, with an eerie moaning sound, it dropped abruptly, twigs shattering in an explosion of sharp cracks.

"Garrett!" Molly screamed, standing up without thinking, then spreading her arms for balance. The lightning tree had crashed at an angle, the top wedging itself into the branches of a hackberry that stood at the edge of the water. Garret had fallen, and she reached to jerk his pole from the mud, then her own. Seconds later, she was poling toward him.

"I'm all right," he called. "So long as there's no cottonmouths around." He tried to laugh, but she could hear how uneasy he was. She leaned to counter his weight as he rolled onto the raft and lay still, breathing hard. "The jar is safe now, anyway. Nothing could bring that tree down from where it's stuck." He fell silent, and Molly listened to the sound of mosquitoes buzzing in the thickening dusk.

"I have to get home," she said finally. "Or Ma is going to stop letting me come."

Garrett nodded.

Molly poled them to the water's edge, and they pulled the raft out. She looked off through the trees. It was getting too dark to carry the cane back through the woods. "I'll have to leave the cane here until morning."

"We should drag the raft up onto the levee road," Garrett said. "We could hide it along that stretch by your place. You know where the willow grows so thick?"

Molly nodded. "I'll help, but then I have to go." She stared at the raft, then looked up the long slope of the levee, getting an idea. "Hey," she said. "We could put the raft in the river and load it with the cane. Then we could just walk the whole mess along the levee like a dog on a rope. It'll be a lot faster."

"That'd work, I think. We'd only have to carry the cane the last little bit past the willow patch. And it'd sure be easier to let the river do the hauling between here and there."

They set to work, loading the cane on the raft. Then they poled slowly across the backwater, using it as a roadway to the levee. At the water's edge, they unloaded the raft. Leaving the cane on the slope, they dragged the raft up onto the levee road. It was hard, but they managed, then they went back down for the cane.

Molly fashioned a towrope out of her twine, tripling it for strength. She laid her sack beside the stacks of cane and their poles, then they set off. Molly held the twine. The raft came along easily.

"You're smart, Molly," Garrett shouted at her over the sound of the river. She grinned and looked up at the sky. The last of the light was dimming; her mother was going to be upset—but at least now she could say it was bringing the cane home that slowed her down.

The raft butted into the levee, and Molly had to push it out with her foot. Another few steps and it veered into the levee again.

"I'll ride," Garrett said. "I can use my pole to nudge it out now and then so it stops getting stuck."

Before Molly could protest, he was climbing on, settling himself, leaning carefully to pick up his pole. She tugged at the twine. "You're heavy," she yelled, teasing him. She pulled harder. The sudden resistance surprised her; it was as if someone had loaded rocks onto the raft.

"What's wrong?" Garrett asked. He pushed lightly on the levee to move the raft away from the bank.

"Don't!" Molly warned him. She could barely hold the twine now. It was cutting into her palm. "There's a current or something," she said, her feet beginning to slide in the mud. The twine snapped, and she sat down hard, then sprang up, staring as the raft slid away from her. "Your pole!"

Garrett extended it. Molly grabbed the end and hauled backward, but the current that had taken hold of the raft was strong. It was swift and sinuous, its path through the slower water marked with ripples and foam, barely visible in the dying light.

"Let go!" Garrett shouted at her above the sound of the rushing river, but it was too late.

Molly was sliding down into the river, pedaling with her feet in the mud, then as the current jerked her forward, she felt the cold water close over her head.

Chapter Five

The instant Molly surfaced, Garrett rolled sideways into the water, hanging on to the raft rope with his left hand. He grabbed the back of her dress and jerked her toward him. She was coughing, her eyes wide, as he helped her onto the raft. He could feel the current tugging at him as he struggled to crawl up beside her. He twisted one way, then the other, astounded at how far from the levee they had already drifted.

He could hear Molly's voice, and at first he thought she was trying to talk over the din of the water. Then he recognized the rhythm of the Lord's Prayer. He blinked, trying to see upstream, but couldn't. It was very nearly pitch-dark.

Suddenly, the raft jerked to one side, as though a giant hand had pulled it sideways across the water. Then it tilted. The bundles of cane skidded across the logs and into the water. He saw Molly recoil and heard her shout as he dug his fingers into the rough-barked logs, hooking his thumb through the rope that held the raft together.

A sheet of foamy water washed over the raft, and Garrett tightened his grip, glancing at Molly. She was half sitting now, facing away from him, her hands desperately searching for a hold on the rope.

The raft spun halfway around, and Garrett was looking downstream again. He hung on, fighting a sick fear in the pit of his stomach. It had all happened so fast. A sharp pain in his right wrist startled him, and he looked down. His arm was bent awkwardly over his pole. He had hung on to it instinctively.

"Your pole!" he shouted at Molly. "Did we lose it?"

He saw her wrench around, looking wildly to one side, then the other, one hand anchored in the rope. She faced him, grimacing as the raft nosed down-ward, the water lapping up over the cut ends of the logs. When it had leveled out again, she shook her head. "I think so. I can't see it floating."

"I still have mine," he shouted at her, trying to pitch his voice above the crashing roar of the river. He could see Molly struggling to turn around. She lurched dangerously to the side, then righted herself. He freed one hand and reached out, but she wasn't looking at him; she was tugging at something caught beneath her. A second later, he understood. Her sack.

"We still have this," she said, her voice raw and uneven.

"We'll be all right," he shouted, hoping that she couldn't hear how scared he was. He reworked his grip on the raft ropes, trembling so hard he could barely slide his thumb back through.

"How far do you think we've gone?" Molly shouted.

Garrett looked up. It was impossible to see past the top of the levee in the dark. Along the horizon, lightning flickered. The roaring suddenly intensified. Garrett tightened his fingers and looked around, trying to understand what was happening. A brilliant flash of blue-white light snaked across the sky, lighting up the world. Thunder, Garrett realized. He was hearing thunder above the sound of the river.

Lightning flashed again, and Garrett saw Molly's

face for an instant, strained and scared. The thunder rolled again, just as the raft slewed sideways, slipping down an incline where a strong current from beneath the surface had bulged upward.

"Garrett!"

He saw her arm flail at the air and heard her shout something else that he couldn't understand. She had lost her hold and was half sliding, half rolling toward the water. Garrett lurched forward and caught at her shoulder, dragging her back toward him. She struggled for a foothold on the slippery logs.

Garrett waited until she had steadied herself, then let go. They both lay still for a few moments, and Garrett could hear her ragged breathing, even above the river.

The lightning exploded above them once more. In the stark light, Garrett saw Molly raise her head.

"I want to tie this to the rope," she shouted unevenly, showing him the sack clutched in her right hand. "But you have to hold me steady."

"Ready?" He looped his arm around hers.

She scooted sideways, positioning the bag in front of her. Then she released the rope. Garrett could feel her shaking as she clumsily knotted the bag to the rope. The pitching of the raft forced her to stop three or four times.

In the lightning flashes, Garrett could see a familiar, determined look in her eyes. When she was finished, she shot him a grin that looked out of place on her frightened face. Then she stretched out beside the sack, and he shifted his grip to her shoulder. She wove her fingers into the raft ropes. "Okay," she shouted after a few seconds. "I'm all right now."

Garrett released his hold on her shoulder and turned back onto his stomach, grateful to be able to hang on with both hands again. The raft moved beneath them violently, rising and falling on the water.

Thunder rumbled again, and Garrett flinched, flattening himself against the wet logs. Lightning split the sky. The crack of thunder that followed it was so loud he had to fight the impulse to cover his ears. The river suddenly dropped from under the raft, and they fell straight downward.

Molly screamed, and Garrett cried out. An instant later, the river shoved itself upward again and caught them. Garrett's head snapped forward with the force of their landing, and he felt his teeth clack together painfully.

The sky sparkled with light once more, and the thunder that chased it was almost deafening. Garrett tried to shout to Molly to hang on, but his words were lost in the rising wall of sound that came from the river, the storm, and the sudden sheet of rain that began to fall. The water from the sky was colder than the water that splashed up between the logs of the raft.

Garrett clung to his handhold and blinked, muting the next flash of lightning into a blood-colored glow. It was better that way, less terrifying. He squeezed his eyes tighter, dimming the lightning to a soft gray. But there was nothing he could do to keep the crashing tear of the thunder out of his ears. Once he thought he heard Molly crying and he reached out blindly to squeeze her hand. She moved closer to him, and he was grateful. For a long time he simply pressed himself against the logs, trying to hide from the reaching stark-white fingers of the lightning.

Garrett wasn't sure when the sound of the water changed. He opened his eyes. Astonished, he looked out across the shining surface of the river. He pulled himself forward, propping himself up on his elbows to be able to see better. Molly's head was still down.

The clouds had lifted, and the rain had stopped. Now, shining from the east was a gibbous moon. Its light silvered everything, changing the water from a seething brown to the color of stars.

"Molly!"

At first she didn't respond, and he felt panic shoot through his whole body.

"Molly!" He loosened his grip on the ropes to reach out and shake her gently—but he could not open his hand.

"Molly! Are you all right?"

She stirred, then raised her head. He managed to nudge her shoulder with his numbed fingers. "The storm is over."

She nodded, looking like a child waking from a long night of nightmares. He tried flexing his hand and managed to move his fingers a little. He half-sat, working his thumb back and forth, feeling a tingling beneath his skin. His other hand had to be just as bad, but he was afraid to let go. The water beneath the raft rose and fell, jolting them.

Garrett bent his legs to ease the pressure of the rough logs and reached down to cup his aching hand over his knee. Pressing against his leg, he managed to straighten his fingers and was amazed at how much it hurt.

"How are we ever going to get home?" Molly asked, just loudly enough for him to hear her over the rushing water. He didn't answer her because he had no idea what to say. He was only sure of two things: He did not want to die. He did not want Molly to die.

Chapter Six

Every time the raft bucked and shuddered beneath them, Molly couldn't help imagining the brown water closing over her head again. She could swim, but no one swam well enough to survive in the Mississippi when it was flooded like this. There wasn't one current to fight, there were ten or twenty, all jostling against one another.

Molly squeezed her hands tighter on the rope, then loosened them. She was chilled through. The cold rain had finally let up, but now the wind was rising. Her legs and feet felt almost numb. The rough bark dug into her skin, and she shifted her weight, rolling onto her side as far as she could without loosening her grip on the ropes.

As she lifted her head, she blinked, surprised at the light of the moon. Garrett was sitting up now, holding on with only one hand. He was rubbing his knee, his face contorted with pain.

"Are you hurt?" she asked him, dragging herself into a sitting position.

He shook his head. "No. My hands are just cramped shut."

Molly nodded. She began tightening her own grip, then loosening it again, over and over, trying to work life back into her fingers.

"I'm hungry," Garrett said so quietly, she could barely hear him over the water. Then he straightened. "Look!"

Molly saw a dark shape out of the corner of her eye. She turned and faced upriver, straining to see in the moonlight. Above them, sliding along the contour of current, chasing the raft, was something huge. She stared at the formless silhouette that loomed in the near darkness.

Molly nudged Garrett with her foot. "What is that?"

"I don't know. But whatever it is, I wish we could get farther away from it."

Without thinking, Molly began working her hands

harder. She saw Garrett notice, then he nodded. "Mine are bad, too. I can barely make my muscles work." He raised his right hand and glared at it.

Molly glanced upriver. The dark shape seemed closer. It looked solid enough to be a house, but in the murky moonlight it was hard to tell. Something hit her leg, hard, and she flopped back over, bending her knee to ease her shin.

"I'm sorry," Garrett said. He was wrestling awkwardly with the pole, both hands on the smooth wood.

Molly freed one hand to take hold of his shirttail. He shot her a grateful glance and worked the pole around so that it was pointing upstream. Molly watched him, then raised her eyes and gasped. The dark shape was getting bigger; it was closer.

Molly sat up, clumsily managing to keep one hand on Garrett's shirt and the other on the rope. She doubled her legs beneath her, feeling the dig of the bark as she continued to squeeze the rope in quick, convulsive little jerks. Her hands were both aching now, and she hoped that was a good sign.

Molly heard Garrett curse and she glanced sideways. He was struggling with the pole. She tightened her hand on his shirt as he angled it upward, fighting the movement of the raft. Finally, the pole nearly vertical, he tried to jam one end into the space between two logs near the center of the raft. He couldn't.

"What are you doing?" Molly shouted into the wind. He had risen on his knees, and she was barely able to keep hold of his shirt and the rope at the same time.

Garrett didn't answer except to gesture upstream. Molly turned and could only stare—it was a house, a whole house, floating on its side. And it was really close now. The sharp peak of the roof was facing her. Sticking out like broken bones were pale branches and splintered planks, trapped beneath the slant of the eaves.

Garrett was leveling the pole at the house, and for the first time Molly understood what he was trying to do. If he could hold them away from it, they might be able to maneuver to the side, let it go past. If not, they could get dragged under the roofline.

Molly shifted her hold on Garrett's shirt to his pant legs as he struggled to steady the pole against the logs. His feet were braced widely apart. The pole dipped and wavered, like a heavy spear.

Molly could see the rows of shingles on the roof now, the moonlight glinting off the wet wood. She watched the tip of the pole as Garrett lowered it. It skated along the slant, then caught on the edge of the tin strip that capped the roof.

Suddenly, Garrett slipped and fell. He sprawled, then curled forward, fighting to stay on the raft. The pole dropped, falling flat, rolling across the logs. Molly reached out, and Garrett locked his hand on her wrist, hauling himself back to kneel beside her. She could hear his rasping breath above the river and the wind and the desperate pounding of her own heart.

An instant later, the raft shuddered as the peak of the roof struck it.

"Hang on!" Garrett screamed.

Molly reached for the pole. "But if we can both brace it, we could—"

"No," Garrett shouted at her. "Just hold on!"

Molly pinned the pole beneath her leg to keep it on the raft, then shifted her hands back to the rope. The river pulled them a few feet ahead of the house, then seemed to shove it toward them. The logs jolted, and Molly cried out in pain as they trapped her right hand. She managed to pull it free, but before she could find a new handhold, the house battered the raft again.

Molly wrenched around to face Garrett, feeling the pole grind against her shin. "The hand ax!" She shouted the words into his ear and pushed at his shoulder. He rolled sideways so she could get at the sack.

With Garrett grasping her shoulder, Molly fumbled at the knot. The salt sack was wet through now, and the cloth was stiff. Hands shaking, she finally got it open. She tucked the hand ax beneath her arm as she resecured the sack, then glanced up and saw the confusion on Garrett's face.

At that instant, the house slammed the raft again, and she grabbed at the rope, the hand ax still held beneath her arm. By the time the raft steadied, the pole was sliding free. Garrett lunged after it, and Molly let go of the rope to grab his ankle.

"We can sharpen the end," Molly shouted at him as he dragged it back toward them. He stared at her for a second, then nodded, and she could tell he understood.

"You hold it," Molly yelled, but he was already

turning the pole around, extending the thickest end toward her, his movements crablike as he used first one hand, then the other, keeping hold of the rope as he worked.

The pole braced against his thigh and angled downward at a gentle slant, Garrett looked up into Molly's face as the raft jolted again. They swayed together at the shock, like trees hit by a gust of wind. Molly looked out across the river, steeling herself for what she had to do. The water was endless, dark, hissing and roiling around the drowned house.

"Be careful!" Garrett yelled.

Molly nodded and rose up onto her knees, the bark digging into her skin. She crawled, grasping the hand ax until she was beside him. Working sideways like this, she could swing the ax without hitting Garrett—or her own legs. But here, she couldn't reach the raft ropes—there was no secure place for her to hold on.

As if to reinforce her fear, the river slammed the house into the raft once more. Molly felt Garrett's hand on her back as he doubled over to regain his hold. When he straightened up, he shouted a single word: "Hurry!"

Molly squared her stance, ignoring the bite of the rough bark as she rose up on her knees and lifted the ax. She struck downward at an angle, then struck again. The third time she raised the ax, Garrett rotated the pole so that her next blow cut into fresh wood.

Breathing hard, Molly felt the ax slice into the wood and saw the chips fly upward. Garrett turned it again, and she kept working. The house hit the raft, a quick, unnerving jerk that knocked Molly off balance. She dropped to all fours in time to steady herself against the next jarring blow—but the hand ax skittered across the logs and disappeared into the water.

"Help me!" Garrett was shouting.

Molly stood up, an odd, hollow feeling in her right hand where the solid ax handle had been a moment before. She guided the forward end of the pole as Garrett jammed the sharpened end into a crack between the raft logs. This time it held.

When the house struck them again, Molly had the pole in position to catch beneath the tin strip. She leaned her entire weight onto the pole, keeping it from sliding out of the crack. The raft felt loose and flighty beneath her bare feet, and she gripped the logs with her toes as best she could. When the house fell back a few feet, she repositioned the pole. The next collision pushed the raft a little to one side.

By the fourth time the house rammed into their pole, they had worked their way so far along the roofline that Garrett twisted the pole free. Molly dropped to her knees and anchored one hand to the ropes and the other to his right ankle.

Garrett shoved at the side of the house, poling past the broken, empty windows and the sad ruin of the porch. A moment later, the house was sliding past, riding the swifter current, as the raft veered off into a quieter channel. Molly fell onto the raft and felt Garrett's arm steady her as they huddled together against the chilling wind.

Chapter Seven

The night seemed to last forever, the rain starting and stopping a dozen times. During one lull, Garrett shifted against the logs, straightening his legs. He half-rolled into a sitting position, careful to keep his right leg on the pole. Molly hadn't opened her eyes in a long time. Garrett couldn't imagine sleeping, but she seemed to be at least dozing a little, her hands still tight around the rope.

Garrett released his grip and rubbed at his face. A big welt on his cheek let him know that there were mosquitoes out now. He switched hands and gingerly touched his right shoulder. Though he couldn't remember when, the pole must have hit him hard.

Molly turned without opening her eyes, and

Garrett noticed the sack, half beneath her right arm. If there was twine left, he could tie the pole down. It'd be a relief to be able to stop worrying about it.

Molly stirred again, turning so the sack would be impossible to reach without waking her. Then he remembered the twine Molly had used as a towrope. The water was calmer, but he was afraid to trust the river. Keeping his leg across the pole, and making sure he always had at least one solid handhold, he scooted to the front edge of the raft. A five-foot length of doubled twine was trailing in the water.

He fished it out, using his pocketknife to cut it. Then he folded the blade. He was careful to settle the knife deep in his pocket. His daddy had given it to him, and he was not going to let the damnable river get it.

The twine was stiff, and Garrett was afraid to let go with both hands, so it took a long time for him to get the pole secured to one end of the raft. When he finished, he was tired and his stomach was churning, empty. He put the thought of food aside. There was nothing to do about it.

An odd tapping sound caught Garrett's attention. He turned to stare out over the water and was startled to see a distant line of treetops. Squinting, he looked up. The moon had set; dawn was beginning to gray the sky.

The tapping came again, barely audible above the sound of the water. Garrett turned, switching hands on the rope, careful to keep his balance as the raft rose and fell. There. Something was riding the current almost parallel with the raft. He couldn't tell what it was. It was too small for a boat, and he couldn't see any people. But it wasn't just some loose boards or fence planks.

Garrett glanced down at Molly. "You awake?" he said softly. She didn't move. He turned back to the river. Whatever it was, it was coming a little closer as the currents jostled each other. The water seemed to be moving faster again.

Garrett looked upriver, relieved to see nothing above them but brown water. The tapping started up again, and Garrett strained to get a better look. It was a metallic sound, almost like a toy hammer striking a nail head.

The current suddenly arched beneath them, rising like a giant cat's back. The raft slewed to one side, moving diagonally. It vibrated, the logs shivering under the conflicting forces. Garrett scrambled closer to Molly as she opened her eyes and sat up, startled.

He steadied her with one hand while she flexed her fingers, then gripped the rope once more. She stretched her spine, shrugging her shoulders. "The rain finally quit?"

She said it so matter-of-factly that Garrett found himself smiling at her. Molly was the only person he could think of who could wake up on a raft in the middle of the Mississippi and talk about the weather like she was sitting on her own front porch. "At least for a while," he told her, then started to laugh.

"What's so funny?" she demanded, staring at him.

"You could use a comb."

She made a face at him and raised her hands to push her hair back from her face in a quick motion. Then she grabbed at the rope again. "You aren't exactly Sunday-meeting presentable yourself."

He smiled at her again.

"What's that?" Molly asked, pointing.

Garrett turned to look. The sky had brightened a little, and the squarish shape suddenly made sense. "It's a chest of drawers, floating on its side. A lot of houses must be ruined."

"I hope both of ours are all right. Do you think our levee could crevasse?"

Garrett shook his head, an image of his mother and sisters running through rising water coming into his mind. He blinked and pushed it aside. "No," he said quickly. "The levee has been there a long time, and it's not like the old ones up at Leota or Scott's Landing. It'll hold."

Molly shivered and looked across the water. She smiled in disbelief. "A chest of drawers," she said. "Listen to that. You can hear the brass drawer pulls. They're swinging back and forth."

Garrett nodded. The chest was only about twenty feet away now. "Let's get ahold of it if we can," he said.

Molly turned to face him. "Why?"

He shrugged. "Maybe we could break it apart— use the pieces for paddles."

Molly arched her brows and smiled. "And the river is going to do the work this time, I think." She gestured toward the chest of drawers. "It's closer already."

Garrett crawled to the edge of the raft and felt Molly grasp his shirttail. "You be careful."

"I will."

The words were barely out of his mouth when the raft nosed downward, carried along a steep wall of water. Garrett flopped back over, clawing for the rope. His fingers snagged on it, and his hands convulsed into fists as he hung on.

The raft began to spin, and Molly shouted something at him, but he couldn't understand. The vortex of the current roared around them, and Garrett looked up. He blinked, unable to understand how the brown water had so quickly shaped itself into a funnel. He had to look *up* to see the surface of the river.

As he watched, transfixed, the chest of drawers tumbled over the rim, falling straight downward for a ways, then slanting into a spin, as the raft had done.

Garrett glanced at Molly. Her eyes were closed, and he willed her to hang on. Then he closed his own eyes, sickened at the sight of the impossible wall of water. He could hear Molly's rasping cry as the raft tilted; it seemed to blend with the whirling motion of the current.

Then, as abruptly as it had begun, the spinning of the raft slowed and finally stopped as it leveled out. Garrett opened his eyes. Molly was flat on her stomach, her face buried in the crook of one arm. He nudged her gently with one foot, still too afraid to let go of his handhold.

Molly sat up, her rose-brown skin an ashen color. "I want to go home."

Garrett waited patiently as she sniffled a little, then apologized for wailing like a baby. He wanted to say something comforting to her, but everything he thought of sounded plain foolish. He couldn't say if they were going to get off the river all right or not. He couldn't tell her he wasn't scared half out of his wits. He could only sit silently as she pulled in one deep breath after another. Finally, she pointed. "There's your chest of drawers."

Garrett followed her gesture, glad to hear her voice sounding steadier, more like her usual self. The river was playing tricks again. Somehow, the chest had gotten ahead of them, but not very far. It was floating even lower in the water now too.

"Hold my ankle, Molly," he said and waited until she had blinked twice, then nodded. Then he stretched out on his belly and began to drag himself toward the front of the raft. At the edge he stopped, staring straight down into the murky water. How deep was it here? His daddy had told him that in some places the Mississippi was as deep as fifty feet. The thought caught at his heart, and for a second, he couldn't breathe. Then he looked up and very nearly banged his nose on the side of the chest.

"Can you get it?" Molly was shouting.

Garrett reached out a cautious hand. The drawers were facing him now, in an uneven row, each one open, the way Ivy and Mae left their chest after they had rifled through it looking for a toy or a doll's shirt. Except that this chest was much finer than anything Mae and Ivy would ever have.

Garrett closed his fingers around a drawer pull and scrooched backward a foot or so. He had to tug pretty hard, but the drawer slid out farther. He jerked at it, and it came free, rattling onto the raft. He sat up quickly, jackknifing around to lay the drawer between him and Molly. Hands shaking, he reached for the rope and clutched it—but this time the river stayed steady beneath them.

Garrett stared at the smooth oak wood and wondered how much perfectly good furniture was floating down the river. His mother would have given anything for a chest of drawers as nice as this one.

As he watched, the chest tilted to one side, floating unevenly now. It sank deeper into the water, and the raft bumped it once, then went past it. Garrett could see just the top of the chest as it fell behind them, then disappeared from sight.

"I wish we could have taken it home," Molly said wistfully, echoing his thoughts.

Garrett shook his head. "It would have just warped to pieces, as soaked as it was." Loosening one hand, he began to examine the drawer. It was shallow, only about four or five inches deep. The front and back were six-inch planks of heavy oak. The drawer bottom was thinner wood. He gripped the brass pull and twisted. It stayed firm. He sat up, holding hard to the rope with his left hand.

"I wish we still had the hand ax. How are you going to break it up?"

Garrett shrugged. He lifted the drawer one-handed, hefting its weight. "I can try to break it against the raft logs," he told Molly. "If I can hit the right angle. Turn your head in case it splinters."

Molly shifted around until her back was toward him. He raised the drawer as high over his head as he could, then smashed it downward, turning it a little so the side of the drawer would hit hardest. There was a satisfying crack, and when Garrett lifted it, he saw that one of the sidepieces had come free. The bottom of the drawer had split in two or three places. He worked it back and forth, widening the biggest crack until the board broke.

It took two more hard whacks, but the front of the drawer finally broke free, the brass pull still firmly attached. It was fit to use as a paddle, as was one of the sidepieces. The remainder of the drawer had been reduced to kindling.

Garrett handed Molly the sidepiece and scooted to the upstream side of the raft. Cautiously, he dipped the drawer front into the water—and it was almost snatched out of his hands. He hung on, skidding, managing to stop only a few inches short of falling into the brown water.

"Not there," Molly yelled. "On the side, like it was a boat."

Garrett nodded and shifted his position again, shaking his head at his own foolish mistake. If he had fallen off the raft . . .

"Can you hear that?" Molly shouted at him over the sound of the water.

Garrett looked at her. "What?"

"I hear a dog barking."

Garrett shook his head, ready to tell her that she was just imagining things—but then he heard it, too. It was more of a howl than a bark, the kind of sound a coon dog made if it was bleeding and hurt, left all alone in the dark.

Chapter Eight

Molly strained to hear, turning one way, then the other. The river had widened out again. The east bank was at least a mile away, and she couldn't see the west bank. The dog had to be on the river, but where?

"Can you spot it?" she shouted at Garrett.

He shook his head. It was getting lighter, and she saw him frown as he craned his neck to look upstream, then down, as she had done. The dog kept howling, but it was impossible to tell where the sound was coming from. The air was too thick with the rushing and rumbling of the river. A mosquito whined close to Molly's face, and she swatted at it.

Abruptly, the dog fell silent, and Molly caught her

KATHLEEN DUEY and KAREN A. BALE

breath. Her imagination produced quick, ugly images of the dog slipping beneath the water's surface. For some reason that made her want to cry more than anything else that had happened. But then the dog began to howl again, and she found herself grinning. She glanced at Garrett, and saw the relief on his face too. It wasn't drowned, at least.

Molly pointed upstream. "You watch that way," she told Garrett and he nodded. Clutching the side-piece from the drawer beneath her right arm, she worked her way to the downstream side of the raft. The day was coming fast; there were pinkish clouds to the south. Molly rubbed at her eyes, then leaned forward again, trying to pinpoint the howling.

A little glimmer of white made Molly tilt her head, staring eastward. It came and went, winking as the sun cleared the horizon. Instantly, there was a shine on the water, a welcome warmth on Molly's skin. The distant shine brightened into a rectangle.

"Is that it?" she shouted, pointing.

Garrett shaded his eyes, and Molly waited. From when they were little, he had always been able to see farther than she had. She watched his face until he smiled and nodded. "I see the dog. It's riding on boards or house siding or something like that. It's smart enough to be lying down."

As the minutes passed, Molly watched the dog closely. It was lying low, its head thrown back to bark. She wondered if it could see them. Maybe if they shouted—no, that might make it stand up, and the next stretch of rough water would be the end of it. As she stared, she realized that the distance between them and the dog was closing. The white planks that carried it were in slower water, a hundred yards or more to the east. "We're going to end up going right by it," she shouted.

"Maybe we can slow the raft down," Garrett yelled back at her. Molly instantly felt the raft react to the dragging pressure of the drawer front. The dog was still pretty far ahead of them, and a long way eastward. She felt the raft crossing the current and grinned at Garrett. "That works like a rudder on a boat. We're turning!"

The dog set up a fresh wail, and Molly shifted so that she could see. Moving at a slant, they were gaining fast. The water was smoother here; the raft wasn't jolting and jumping nearly as much as it had been before.

"I can't hold it much longer," Garrett said.

Molly faced him. "I'll take a turn."

Garrett sighed and lifted the drawer front out of the water. The raft lurched, and he tipped backward, his hands clutching the makeshift paddle. Molly managed to grab his wrist, and they both regained their balance, breathing hard.

"Be more careful," Molly said.

Garrett got his left hand beneath the rope and closed his fist tightly. With his right, he pretended to doff an invisible hat. "Yes, ma'am."

Molly took the drawer front and positioned herself at the rear corner of the raft as he moved forward. She lowered the board slowly and was amazed at how hard it was to control, even using the brass drawer pull as Garrett had done. The current was not only incredibly strong, it fluttered and vibrated the smooth wood. The board was like a live thing just waiting for a chance to break free.

"We're doing pretty well," Garrett shouted to her from his new perch on the front of the raft.

Molly's right arm was trembling with effort when they finally got close to the dog. Its float was slick white-painted planks that looked like they had been torn from the side of a building. They were thin and barely supported the dog's weight. The water sloshed across the boards from both sides, covering its paws most of the time. The poor animal was wet and bedraggled. It was skinny, too, and shivering.

"How are we going to get it onto the raft?" Molly asked Garrett, hoping he had an idea. She sure didn't.

Garrett shook his head. "If we could get up to within a couple feet, we could maybe tie our boards together and the dog could walk across and . . ." He trailed off, looking around. Molly sighed, angry at herself for not keeping an eye on the sidepiece. Somehow the loop of twine had slipped free and it was gone.

"Oh, my Lord." Garrett was staring downriver. Molly turned. There, less than half a mile ahead, she could see a stretch of water whitened with foam. Now that she was looking at it, she heard it, too.

Garrett started shouting at her. "We don't have time for the dog. We have to get as far eastward as we can—maybe we can miss the worst of it." Molly turned to see him gesturing, his face pale.

The dog yowled. It was facing them now, still thirty feet away across the swift, bottomless river.

"We have to help it," Molly yelled at Garrett.

"No!" he screamed back. "There isn't time, Molly. Help me turn the raft."

Molly glanced at the dog once more. It had stood up and was hunched forward, poised at the edge of its planks, eyes fastened on hers. "Come on," she yelled impulsively. "Can you swim? Come on!"

The dog hesitated a few seconds longer, then plunged into the water. Molly gasped as it sank, then came up again, turned the wrong way.

"Over here," Garrett yelled at it. "We're here, come on, you can do it!"

Molly started shouting, too. The dog swam frantically for a moment, headed away from them, then it pivoted in the water, and Molly could see its ears prick up when it saw them. "Swim!" she shouted at it, crossing her fingers.

The dog paddled desperately, crossing the current, its muzzle tipped almost straight up to keep the splashing water out of its nostrils. Its paws flashed, lifting completely out of the water at times when the current shifted, falling from beneath it. Slowly, panting and wild-eyed, the dog closed the distance between them.

It's going to make it, Molly thought. *It really is!* She started to move toward the dog, anchoring one hand so that she could lean out to help it.

"Molly!" Garrett screamed from behind her.

She glanced up. The rough water was just ahead of them. In seconds, the raft would begin to leap and jolt. She turned to the dog. It was so close now that she could see its whiskers, brown on one side and white on the other. They matched the blotches of color that divided its face.

"Molly!" Garrett screamed again as she leaned out as far as she could, clinging to the rope with one hand. The dog bobbled in the water and went under, coming up a second later, its ears plastered flat, choking. Molly inched toward it, straining. The dog struggled harder, seeing her outstretched hand, its paws working furiously, fighting against the brown water pulling at it from beneath.

Molly glanced ahead. The current was already rougher. She was afraid to lean out any farther. The dog slid beneath the water once more. At that instant, Molly felt Garrett's strong hand on her leg. She didn't look at him, but kept her eyes fixed on the terrified animal, she let go of the rope and leaned outward, reaching with both hands. The dog managed to break the surface once more, and Molly grabbed the loose skin on the back of its neck.

Pulling the dog onto the raft, corralling it with her legs as she sat up and reached for the rope, Molly saw Garrett scooting backward across the logs. They had time to exchange a single glance before they hit the rough water.

Chapter Nine

The first jolt knocked Garrett backward. The second was worse. He heard the dog yelp and Molly shout— not words, just a loud cry. He managed to roll over and wedge the side of one foot down into a crack between two of the raft logs, pinning the drawer front beneath him. He struggled to hang on, lifting his head to see Molly.

She had fallen sideways across the raft and was clawing at the logs with her right hand, trying to find the rope. Her left arm was doubled around the dog, clutching it awkwardly against her body. The dog looked terrified, but it was still, not fighting Molly's grip.

"I've got you," Garrett yelled as he stretched out

and captured her wrist. A moment later, with him guiding her, Molly found the rope. The drawer front was digging into Garrett's side, and he shifted his weight to ease the sharp pain.

The raft was shuddering now, crashing through hummocks of water, capped by white foam and early sunlight. Sheets of water fanned over them, and Garrett longed to wipe his eyes but was afraid to. The raft bounced and jittered, and he clenched his jaw, blinking, watching Molly as well as he could. She was managing to hold on with one hand, but he could see the effort it was costing her. Her face was contorted into a fierce frown. Garrett loosened his grip to reach beneath himself and reposition the drawer front. Then he closed his hand around the rope again. Molly's frown had become a grimace.

"Give the dog to me," he shouted at her.

Her eyes had been closed, but now she opened them long enough to meet his stare and shake her head. "If it gets away," she yelled back, "it'll drown."

Garrett was about to answer when the raft tilted so steeply that Molly and the dog were perched above him for a second, silhouetted against the blue sky. Then they crashed back down as the raft righted itself. The dog yelped as the raft hit the surface of the water. Garrett was afraid the terrified animal would snap at Molly's face, inches from its own, but it didn't. It stood beside her, her left arm around its belly. Its paws were splayed out as it fought for balance.

The rough water went on a long time, the raft hammering against the uneven currents. Garrett saw Molly struggling to keep hold of the dog, but there was nothing he could do to help her. One smashing jolt followed the next so closely that he had no time to reset his grip on the rope, to do anything but hang on. The water beneath the raft was so turbulent that it spewed up between the logs, cold and dark.

When the water finally calmed a little, Garrett found himself curled up around the drawer front, both hands tangled in the rope, his whole body shaking. He straightened his legs and turned over, afraid that Molly would not be there—but she was. And so was the dog.

He looked down to see the drawer front sliding across the logs and he immediately pulled it back, amazed that he had forgotten it. Without it, they had no way to steer the raft.

"Are you all right?" Garrett shouted at Molly. His voice sounded too loud now that the water was quieter. The sun was well up. How much time had gone by while they had been caught in the rough water?

She turned to look at him. "I think so." She scooted into a half-sitting position, and Garrett saw streaks of blood on her legs from the rough bark. The dog scrambled on the slick logs, and Molly loosened her hold on it, murmuring comforting nonsense to calm it down.

"We have to find it something to eat," Molly said, looking up.

"For ourselves, too," Garrett added. He released both hands long enough to stretch. Then he picked up the drawer front in his right hand and took hold of the rope again with his left. He watched the water in front of the raft. It was much calmer here, and he was sure they were out of the river course now. They somehow had ended up east of the levees, floating above flooded farmland. There were hundreds of rounded treetops sticking up out of the brown water.

"I'm going to try to turn the raft again," he told

Molly. "If we go far enough eastward, maybe we can find a place to get up out of the river."

Molly was fussing with the dog's coat, rubbing at it the way a mother would warm a chilled child. She looked up long enough to nod at him. "You need help?"

Garrett shook his head. "I don't think so. No, not here. If the water gets rough again, I will."

All of a sudden the dog yipped, lifting its muzzle to bark at the sky. Then it stood up and shook, droplets flying into Garrett's face. Molly turned her head, laughing. Garrett found himself smiling, too. There was something so everyday about the dog shaking that the idea of them being in the middle of the flood, who knew how far from home, was almost funny. Garrett's laughter died when he saw a look of sadness cross Molly's face.

"How can we laugh when we don't even know if our own families are alive?"

He shrugged, confused by how angry her words made him. He scooted closer to the back edge of the raft. "Hang on to the dog, but you keep a tight hold on the rope, too."

He lowered the smooth wood into the water, using the drawer pull as a grip. He did it slowly this time, and the raft responded without jerking. Molly turned to flash a smile at him, and he felt his anger dissolve. The dog sat down beside her, huddling companionably against her side.

The drowned trees gradually drew nearer. The farther they got from the main channel of the river, the slower the water moved. The slower it moved, the quieter it got. Garrett felt odd in the silence. Molly sighed, and he could hear her clearly. From a distance, he heard birdsong. The world had become calm again.

The water was too muddy to tell how deep it was, but as they glided close to the first of the trees, Garrett looked up to see a mockingbird's nest only five feet above his head. The mother bird glared and jabbered at him until he was well past.

It was odd, floating silently into the high branches like this. He wondered what was beneath the raft, covered by the brown water. Someone's house? A barn full of dead mules and drowned chickens? A family?

"Where do you suppose we are?" Molly asked quietly.

Garrett shrugged. "We've come a ways, that's for sure. Maybe we're clear down past Ben Lommond, or all the way to Shiloh."

Molly tilted her head, listening. "Do you hear someone hollering?"

Garrett listened hard for a full minute, then shook his head. "If they were, they've quit now."

"What are we going to do?" Molly pushed her hair back with both hands.

Garrett met her eyes. "Get to land and find help, I guess."

Molly had let go of the dog and was sitting with her hands in her lap. Garrett realized that there was almost no pressure on the drawer front, and he lifted it out of the water and laid it on the raft. He stretched, arching his back, aware of every tired muscle, every bruise. He lifted his face toward the incredible warmth of the sun. He had been chilled so long that he could almost feel the cold seeping out of him into the warm morning air. Mosquitoes hummed around them.

"This is like heaven," Molly said softly, and he nodded, understanding her perfectly. The water here was not trying to kill them.

He crawled across the raft, gently nudging the dog to one side. Hoping it was shallow enough, he untied his pole and slid it downward. He tried angling it one way, then the other. Nothing. He worked it deeper, pushing it an arm's length beneath the surface, but it was no good. The water was calm, but it was still too deep.

"Wish we had a motor," he said sadly, rocking back on his heels. He put the pole next to the drawer front, then lay on his back, wincing.

"I wish we had breakfast." Molly's voice was soft and wistful. The dog whined quietly as if it had understood her. "I'm sorry I lost my paddle."

"I almost lost mine. You saved the dog. It'd be a pretty one if it weren't so rail-thin. Maybe we can get it all the way home with us."

Molly nodded. "Maybe. Pa would probably let me keep it." She touched the dog's shoulder. It moved closer so that she could scratch its ears.

Garrett lay flat, letting the raft drift through the trees. He closed his eyes against the dappled sunlight, wishing for food and a softer bed, but grateful to be alive and away from the murderous current.

"What's that sound?" Molly asked.

Garrett listened. He could just hear something above the distant roar of the water. It took his tired mind a moment to recognize it, but when he did, he sat bolt upright. "Airplane!" He grabbed the drawer front and started paddling. "They'll be looking for people stuck on the river."

The drawer front made a poor paddle at best. It was hard to hold and harder to guide, but he got the raft moving slowly back toward the open river. The sound of the airplane grew louder and louder. Molly was turning, neck craned and one hand shading her eyes. "I think I see it. The sun is glinting off something!"

Garrett lowered his head and put every ounce of his strength into paddling. It was almost impossible to make the raft go straight, and he had to keep scooting from one side to the other. The dog jumped out of his way, barking at him once or twice. Molly tried to quiet it, then began using her hands to paddle, trying to help.

When the airplane roared overhead, they were still under the trees. Molly jumped to her feet, waving her hands and shouting. Garrett staggered up to stand beside her, rumbling at the buttons on his shirt, peeling it off to wave it in a futile circle above his head, shouting at the top of his lungs.

The plane flew straight on, following the river. The sound of the engine faded.

Chapter Ten

Molly sat down, watching Garrett sink to his knees. "Put your shirt on," she said gently. "You'll get a chill." His face bleak, he didn't answer her. She patted the dog, searching for something else to say. "There'll be another plane, won't there? I mean, if they're flying along here, there'll be another one soon, probably."

Garrett raised his eyes and nodded vaguely. He shook out his shirt and slid it back on. He kept glancing at the sky, and Molly chided herself again for letting her piece of the drawer get away. If she had been able to paddle, too, maybe they'd have gotten out of the trees in time to be seen. Garrett was lying down again, his eyes closed. He looked blanched, weary.

Molly wriggled her toes, looking at the scrapes

and cuts on her legs. "What do you think we ought to do now?"

"Nothing."

Molly stared at him. "What do you mean?"

He opened his eyes and frowned. "We have one stupid little board to paddle with. And look." He raised up on one elbow and showed her his right palm. The edges of the drawer front had raised big, ugly blisters beneath his skin.

Molly watched him lie back and close his eyes again. He had deep scratches all over his hands and arms. His right cheek was skinned raw and smeared with blood.

The dog whined and pushed its head against her shoulder. Molly hugged it, fighting a dark feeling that was creeping into her heart. They hadn't come through the whole terrible night to just give up, had they?

Molly picked up the drawer front, sliding her hand through the pretty brass pull. The dog whined again, but moved away to let her stand up. She placed her feet carefully, taking small steps, lowering herself slowly, to sit on the back edge of the raft. She knew Garrett was awake, had felt the raft rock when she moved—but he didn't say anything.

The dog settled itself beside her. Molly lowered the makeshift paddle into the water. She tried to make a long, smooth stroke, but she had put the drawer front in too deeply and very nearly tipped herself into the water.

Molly kept trying. The raft started to turn in a circle, and she shifted to change the thrust of her paddling. After a few minutes of getting nowhere at all, she managed to straighten the raft out and move it forward. Garrett lay silently as she worked.

Molly paddled them out from beneath the trees, then started them downstream again, staying far to the edge of the current. She sat still once the raft was moving steadily, the drawer front acting like a rudder again, steering a rough course in the brown water. The last thing she wanted was to end up in the swift torrent of the main channel again.

She headed eastward as much as she could. Somewhere, the flood had to end. There had to be a place where the river got shallow, then stopped, and dry land began again. But as she guided the raft along, all she could see was brown water stretching in every direction, lying cold and heavy on the land.

Molly kept an eye on Garrett and, after an hour

or so, she was pretty sure he had really fallen asleep. "Let him rest," she said to the dog. It pricked up its ears and tilted its head. "He worked harder than I did this morning," Molly told it, grateful for its attention, its bright eyes.

She stared to the east as they slowly curved into a wide, gentle turn, following one of the great loops in the river course. She pushed the drawer front deeper, canting it more severely, moving the raft across the sluggish current. She sat tensely. It was impossible to say how the currents would switch and shift as the river turned.

The bend in the river seemed to go on forever. Molly listened, fearful, half-expecting to hear the deep roar of angry water straight ahead. The Mississippi was full of tricks.

Molly's tension eased when the raft came slowly around the last of the curve and she could see the calm water stretching out for miles in front of her. The worst of the current was still safely to the west somewhere. She could hear it only if she listened hard. Garrett stirred slightly and she smiled, wishing he would wake up so she could brag about getting them this far safe and sound, but he didn't.

The sun was getting hotter. Molly squinted, hoping to see a line of trees, or the grassy top of a levee. Her legs were cramped and aching, and she sighed, thinking about being able to get off the raft. After a few minutes, she spotted something and shaded her eyes.

It was hard to tell, but it looked like there was an island in the distance, or maybe it was just a tangle of wood or another floating house or something. Molly shifted the drawer front, trying to turn the raft harder. She judged the direction, constantly readjusting, then squinting to try to make out enough detail to know what she was headed for.

With every minute that passed, Molly guided the raft farther from the river's normal channel, farther into flood water. The current got weaker, until the raft was barely moving. She tried paddling again, but Garrett had been right. The smooth wood was deceptively sharp edged, and the pain in her hand was impossible to ignore after fifteen or twenty strokes.

Molly gave up paddling. The dog left her side to curl up by Garrett, resting its head on its front paws. She nodded at it. "You two just take a nap, then. I surely don't mind."

Neither the dog nor Garrett responded in any

way. Molly looked past them. The course of the raft was about perfect now. Molly steered as the sluggish current moved them forward. It *was* a patch of high ground, maybe one of the old Indian mounds. Pa said there were a lot of them all through the Delta. Molly glanced at Garrett, resisting an urge to wake him up. She would wait until she had the raft right up against dry ground, then she'd surprise him. He was going to be proud of her.

As the raft swayed gently, Molly found herself yawning, in spite of the sharp hunger pains in her belly and the aching of her cramped muscles. The high ground drew slowly closer, and she could see what looked like shade trees on one side, and the gray-green of early cabbage plants in a garden on the other. She couldn't see a house, but there probably was one, deep under the magnolias. The shade looked enticing. Her backside ached as she thought about being able to sit down on soft grass instead of hard, uneven wood.

Molly picked up the drawer front and began to paddle again, slowly, careful not to grip the edge so tightly that it grated against her skin. The current picked up a little.

As she got closer, she decided that it probably was an Indian mound. It looked like the ones south of Mayersville, anyway. There were drowned trees all around it, some with just a branch or two raised above the surface.

Garrett and the dog were both still sound asleep when Molly spotted the old cabin. So this was just high ground, she thought, not an Indian mound. The cabin was a sprawling affair, like many old-timers' places were. One end had a white planked porch. The other, squatty and dark, was made of notched logs. Probably the porch had been added on recently.

Molly switched the makeshift paddle from one hand to the other, arching her back to relieve her tired muscles. To the west, out of the corner of her eye, she saw an odd brown-gray ripple in the water. She half-turned, her eyes fixed on the movement. She tried hard to believe that it was just a stray tendril of the main current, or a breeze-ruffle on the water, or a stick that had worked itself free from the main channel. But she knew it wasn't. It was a snake.

Molly sat transfixed, staring. Like all cottonmouths, it swam with a menacing grace, its wedge-shaped head just above the water. Molly had seen a pig die once, a two-hundred-pound sow, blue and swollen from a cottonmouth bite.

Molly watched the snake, the hair on the back of her neck prickling a little. A cottonmouth in the water was a dangerous thing—even worse than on the ground.

The snake seemed to be swimming parallel to the raft. Molly back-paddled a little, hoping that it would just go on downriver. If it swam far enough the way it was going now, it'd probably see the island, too. She didn't want to have to watch out for it—though seeing it like this was probably a good reminder that all the high ground would be infested with snakes.

Molly kept back-paddling, one eye on the cotton-mouth. She could not seem to slow the raft enough to let it go past. She paddled faster, uneasy. Had the distance between her and the snake shortened? Molly wiped a sheen of sweat from her forehead. It had. She stared, swallowing hard. It looked like the snake was coming *toward* her now.

Molly began to paddle harder. Maybe it was just trying to find the edge of the submerged land and a dry place to sleep. If she got a little ahead of it, it might pass behind the raft. If it did, Molly was pretty sure she could still turn the raft in time to make landfall.

The snake lifted its head a little higher out of the water, and Molly froze as it turned to look straight at her, then lowered its head again. When it began to swim once more, it was coming right at her.

"Garrett?" Her voice sounded tremulous and weak in her own ears. He blinked and groaned. The dog shifted, but didn't waken. "Garrett!"

This time he opened his eyes fully and rolled onto his side. "What?"

Molly tore her eyes from the snake for an instant. "Cottonmouth!" She pointed.

Garrett rolled forward into a squatting position. For an instant, he did nothing more. Then he exploded into motion. He grabbed the pole and got to his feet. Startled, the dog jumped up and turned a quick circle, growling. "Hold on to the dog," Garrett said in a tense, low voice. He shoved the pole down into the water, his face rigid with determination, his knuckles white from the intensity of his grip. But the pole plunged downward without resistance. The bottom was out of reach. He shot Molly a look. "Paddle!"

Molly leaned forward, grabbing the scruff of the dog's neck and dragging it toward her. She held it close with her right hand, her left gripping the drawer front. She paddled one-handed, awkward and frantic.

"It's coming right at us," Garrett rasped.

Molly watched the snake arch up out of the water, opening its white-lined mouth as it came closer. The dog growled low in its throat, and the hair along its back bristled.

"Stay clear of the pole," Garrett shouted. "And keep the dog away."

Molly dropped the drawer front and grabbed at the dog. Startled, it snarled at her, then wrenched around in her arms to face the snake, the hair down its spine a ridge of fear. Garrett was raising the pole at an angle, his whole body tense. The snake came closer. Molly could see it sliding through the water, weaving effortlessly back and forth. The sunlight glinted off the silent ripples it left behind.

Molly snatched up the board again and paddled as well as she could without letting go of the dog. Garrett widened his stance, and Molly held her breath as he lowered the pole, poking at the snake. It turned aside, and she exhaled in relief. Then it rolled in the water and came toward them again.

"Go on!" Garrett said, pushing the end of the long pole beneath the snake's belly. "Leave us alone!" Garrett lifted the pole and swung it, trying to throw the snake aside, but the cottonmouth flowed over the pole, sliding silently back into the water. It drew itself up, its unblinking eyes fixed on the raft. The dog sprang forward, and Molly hauled it back, its paws scrabbling on the wet logs as it struggled against her.

Garrett jabbed at the snake. It rose a little higher out of the water, and Molly could hear it hissing as it waited for the pole to strike again. Garrett managed once more to get the pole beneath the snake, but it simply slid over it and down into the river again.

Molly watched, horrified, as Garrett stepped back. The snake kept coming, bumping its head lightly along the edge of the raft, slithering into the crack between the two center logs. The dog went crazy, barking, stiff legged, its eyes rimmed in white. Molly let go of it and took up the drawer front in both hands.

"Wait!" Garrett yelled. He raised the pole and drove it downward, trying to shove the sharpened end deep into the crack. The snake writhed and hissed, knotting up, then struck, barely missing Garrett's leg. The dog lunged forward, then danced backward as the snake regathered itself and struck again. Garrett lurched sideways, losing his balance. He fell into the water, his arms wide, his face contorted with fear.

Reflexively, Molly reached out to him and saw the snake turn its head toward her. The dog jumped in front of her, and Molly raised the slender board that was the only weapon she had. Snarling, the dog snapped at the snake, then jumped aside when it struck. Molly began working her way around the side of the raft. She could hear Garrett choking on the dirty water, thrashing beside the raft, but she couldn't take her eyes from the snake for even an instant.

The dog barked, stiffening when the snake opened its ugly, white-lined mouth. Molly could see its fangs. She raised her plank above her head, staring at the snake, waiting. When it struck, she brought her board down with all her strength, slamming the snake's head against the logs. The dog darted forward in that instant and sank its teeth into the snake's body, then leaped away. The snake whipped around to face it, giving Molly time to raise her board. This time, her blow landed just as the snake was shrinking backward from the dog's snarling advance.

The board hit corner-first, a few inches behind the snake's head. The snake writhed, trying to slide farther into the crack between the logs. Molly jammed the board against it, trying to pin its head. It struggled wildly, lashing its body back and forth. Molly shrieked when it wrapped itself around her leg, but she didn't allow herself to flinch. The force of her weight on the drawer front didn't waver. The long, muscled body flung itself in a high arc, thrashing against the smooth oak board that pinioned its head relentlessly against the log.

"Here!"

Molly glanced sidelong to see Garrett clinging to the side of the raft, the open sack near his hand. He was holding out the knife. "You have to do it. If I try to climb up, the raft'll tip and you'll lose it."

Molly nodded, stretching out her hand to take the knife. Her whole body was trembling, vibrating with fear. "Keep the dog back," she managed to say.

Garrett nodded gravely. "I will."

She saw him move off, pulling himself along the edge of the raft. She heard him calling the dog, but then, her whole mind focused on what she had to do.

Leaning hard on the board, Molly worked herself into position above the snake. It struggled even harder than it had at first. When it hit her legs, it hurt like a broom handle.

She bent over the snake, resting much of her weight on the board, her breath coming in quick spurts, her legs shaking with fear. She gripped the knife handle hard and placed the blade on the snake's neck. Then, with sudden, terror-driven pressure, she sawed at it.

The snake reacted to the first touch of the knife, whipping itself against the logs. Even once its head had been severed, the convulsions went on, and Molly stood up, still shaking, afraid to let go of the board.

"Molly, hang on! I'm coming up."

The raft tipped to one side, and Molly squatted to keep her balance as Garrett clambered on. For the first time, she noticed the dog was still barking. The bloody knife clattered from her fingers onto the logs. Garrett was prying her hand from the board, talking quietly as though she were a spooked colt. "You did it, Molly. You did it. It's dead."

Molly felt something cool brush her cheek and she shrank away, startled. Garrett pointed upward, and she followed his gesture. The clouds had covered the sun. It was starting to rain again.

Chapter Eleven

Garrett picked up the knife and used it to flip the severed snake head into the water. Then he eyed the still-convulsing body as he put the knife back in the sack and tied it shut. The snake's muscles would continue to spasm for a half hour or more. Rain was beading on the smooth gray-brown scales. "Maybe we should keep it. If we could just make a fire somewhere—" He pushed the dog aside firmly and shook a finger in its face. "You hush now." He looked over his shoulder at Molly. "We could skin it and eat it." She didn't answer him.

The dog had quieted, still staring at the headless snake. Still bristling, it came forward, lowering its muzzle.

"Hey, Garrett."

He glanced at Molly. She was pointing. He turned to look. A hundred yards off was a little hump of land sticking up out of the muddy water. There were trees hanging over a low-slung old house. Through the rain, Garrett thought he saw a wisp of smoke rising from the chimney. He glanced at Molly.

"I was going to surprise you," she said, shivering. She sank onto the logs and leaned over the side of the raft to wash her hands in the water. "I thought maybe we could see what's in the house. Maybe they left some food behind."

Garrett squinted. "Somebody is still there. I can see smoke."

Molly wiped at her face. "Maybe they'll let us come in and get warm."

Garrett nodded, turning to grab the drawer front. He went to the back of the raft and sat down, a rivulet of rain running from his hair down his shirt. "If you sit on that side, we can take turns. These blisters are pretty bad."

He flexed his right hand as Molly sat down opposite him. Trading off every four or five strokes, they moved the raft steadily over the nearly still water.

The dog was still nosing at the snake, snuffling and growling.

"Get away," Molly called to the dog. "I'm not going to eat it after you get finished drooling all over it." Garrett nudged the dog with his foot. It went to lie down near Molly.

"It's an old place, I think," Molly said as they got closer.

Garrett nodded. "It sure looks like one." He could see a path on one side that rose up out of the water and looked like it led to the house. "Aim for that," he said to Molly, gesturing. He dragged the paddle to turn the raft slightly, grimacing as his blisters stung. When they traded off again, Molly kept the same course.

They bumped into the soft dirt, only five or six feet to one side of the path. The dog jumped past Garrett and sprang off the raft. Garrett could see sharp tracks in the soft dirt. This trail had been worn by cows' hooves.

Garrett glanced back out over the water. Where was the barn? It was strange to think that a whole farm except for the house had been covered by water, but that was probably what had happened here.

"Maybe we should call out, first," Molly cautioned, standing with her arms out for balance as the raft settled against the shoreline. "They can hardly be expecting company."

Garrett cupped his hands around his mouth. "Helllooooo!" He stepped onto the dirt, his legs stiff and clumsy. The ground felt too solid, strange, and immobile beneath his feet. Molly jumped off, bumping into him from behind. Together they dragged the raft above the waterline. Molly opened the sack and fashioned a short tie-rope out of the twine.

"I think it'll hold. What about the snake?"

Garrett bent to tug at the twine. It was as strong as they could make it. "Leave it here for now. If there's any choice, I don't want to eat it."

"Me either," Molly said as she followed him up the path.

Garrett stopped and whistled for the dog. It came bursting out of a plum thicket, and Molly grabbed at it as it went past. She kept it close as they stepped into the yard. Garrett shouted again. This time he heard a voice from inside.

He glanced at Molly, noticing the mad tangle of her hair and the mud stains on her dress. He could hardly look any better. He ran his fingers through his hair and nudged Molly. She straightened her dress and pulled her hair back, then stood up, squaring her shoulders.

"You look pretty good for a half-drowned snake-killer," he said in a mock-serious voice. Molly flashed him one of her quick grins. Then the house door banged open hard enough to rattle the front window.

"Who is that? Who is calling out there?"

Garrett stepped forward so that the man could see him clearly. "Me and Molly here got washed downriver on our raft, sir. We surely didn't mean to give you a start."

The man stared, then laughed aloud. "Son, my house is the only thing above water for miles. All my neighbors have run for high ground at Vicksburg. I've seen fifteen snakes, two gators, and a floating church. It'd take more than two muddy children and a mutt to give me a start."

Garrett smiled, expecting the man to return it, but he didn't. The dog broke free of Molly's grip and ran up to the man, slinking low as it got close, begging for attention. The man bent down and patted its skinny side. "You ought to feed your dog better, boy," he said as he scratched the dog's ears.

"It's not mine," Garrett told him. "We found it on the river. Molly nearly drowned saving it."

The man straightened, looking at Molly. "A lot of folks would leave a dog to die." He continued to stare at them. When he spoke again, his voice was a little friendlier. "I suppose, since you're here, the polite thing is to ask you in."

Once again Garrett smiled, and once more the man did not respond. "We have a dead snake on the raft," Garrett said. "A big cottonmouth. If you have a fire, we could—"

But the man was already shaking his head. "I will eat gator. I will eat armadillo. I will eat squirrel and possum and coon. I will not eat snake."

Garrett shifted his weight from one foot to the other, blinking rain out of his eyes. The man was really old, he realized, in spite of his forceful voice. He was leaning on the porch rail.

"We would surely appreciate a little something to eat, Mister," Molly said in a quivery voice. Her teeth were chattering.

There was a small, awkward silence, then the old man took a half step backward. "Come in out of the rain, then." The dog followed at his heels.

Garrett led the way across the muddy yard past a slant-roofed shed. There were fig trees off to one side of the house, and a stand of blackberries grew along the other. The place was neat and well kept. There was a little patch of strawberries in a box planter, with a woven-cane lattice set up to keep animals out.

At the bottom of the house steps, Garrett hesitated, waiting for Molly to catch up. Her eyes were wide with interest as she passed the strawberry bed. "That's sure pretty," she said, pointing.

The old man ignored her and banged the door open again. He went inside without a backward glance, the dog right behind him.

"Why is he so unfriendly?" Molly whispered as Garrett opened the door. Garrett shrugged, touching one finger to his lips. Molly nodded, and they stepped in out of the rain.

Garrett blinked. The inside of the house was dimly lit. There was a low fire in a massive stone hearth, and a candle sitting in a tin can on a table. The dog circled twice, then lay down in front of the fire. Garrett saw an electric light fixture on the ceiling. "The rain knock out your Delco plant?" he asked.

"No," the old man replied instantly. "It was a flock of white crows." He gestured toward the front window. "Came flyin' in yesterday about sunup."

Garrett felt a wave of anger rise inside him at the old man's teasing. "Mister, we are about as tired and cold and hungry as we can be. We didn't mean to barge in on you like this, but—"

"No, son," the man interrupted, going to stand before the fire. "You are not nearly as wet and cold and tired as you might be." The orangish light made the creases in his face look deep, each one a dark line. He crossed his arms, and Garrett noticed that his right hand was missing most of its fingers.

"The stew's been cooking all day," the old man said. He went to a cupboard and took out three mismatched china bowls.

"How long have you been here alone?" Molly asked, moving to stand nearer the fire. Garrett tried to signal her. This old man didn't seem to want much conversation. But Molly either didn't see his gesture or she ignored it.

"You have family, Mister?"

Garrett waited for the old man to snap at Molly and tell them to take their nosy business back out to their raft—but he didn't. He just began dishing up the stew. Once they each had a full bowl and a spoon, they sat cross-legged on the floor by the fire.

Then the old man settled back into his easy chair, facing the hearth. He stirred his stew noisily, blowing at it to cool it off. Outside, the rain fell harder, a sleepy thrumming on the roof.

"I did have a big family," the old man said quietly. "Outlived all but three. My son is up in Greenville. My brother and his wife went out to California in twenty-one. I got a letter at Christmas. They have an orange tree in their yard out there."

Garrett watched Molly nodding, her eyes big as she imagined the orange tree. He took a bite of the stew and scalded his tongue. The dog raised its head, then rested it on its front paws, sniffing at the warm odor of onions and meat.

"You ever go visit out there?" Molly was asking in between bites.

"Once," the old man said. "It's a long trip for old bones."

Molly nodded at that, too. Garrett blew on a mouthful of stew, then gulped it down. The chill from the rain was leaving him, and he stopped shivering.

The old man was still stirring and blowing. "Where are the two of you from, then?"

Molly nudged Garrett, and he cleared his throat. "Mayersville, sir."

"Mayersville," the old man said, as though Garrett had named some grand city. "I've never been up that way. The war mostly took me South."

Garrett stared at him. Mr. Talbot had fought in the Great War over in Europe. So had Bubba Lawlor. Neither one of them even had gray hair yet. Suddenly, Garrett realized what the old man meant. "You fought in the War between the States?"

The old man nodded. "I did. Ended up with Lieutenant General Pemberton at Vicksburg. And he had true Southern blood, no matter what they say."

Garrett felt Molly stiffen. He was unsure what to say or do. A spatter of rain hit the front window.

"My family never owned a slave," the old man said, staring into the fire. "We were poor and proud to do our own work. But I hated that government in Washington telling us what to do. If they had left us alone—"

"Is that what happened to your hand?" Garrett blurted out, hoping to turn the conversation away from slavery.

"Gun misfired," the old man said. "We surely lost that war. I doubt ol' Dixie will ever recover." The old man sat quietly after he finished talking, stirring the bowl of stew.

"My mama says President Coolidge could fix us up with farm relief," Garrett said into the silence that had gathered in the room.

"Maybe," the old man said. "Maybe not. It'd take a whole lot of relief to put Warren County to rights."

The only sound was the snapping of the fire and the muted bubbling of the stew pot. Garrett finished eating and set his bowl on the hearth. The dog whimpered. The old man stopped stirring and stuck his thumb straight down into the stew.

"Cool enough." He leaned to set the bowl in front of the dog. It scrambled to its feet and began lapping at the stew. Garrett kept glancing at Molly, wondering what she was thinking. If this old man had won his war, she might have been born a slave.

"Mayersville is up in Issaquena County, isn't it?" the old man asked.

"Yes," Garrett told him. "Up around Rolling Fork." Molly set down her dish, her eyes clouded and distant.

"I reckon you two are about seventy, eighty miles from home, then. You're not all that far from Vicksburg."

Garrett heard Molly pull in an astonished breath. He realized he had opened his own mouth and closed it, not knowing what to say. The old man began to laugh. He tilted his head backward, aiming his merriment at the smoke-stained ceiling. He laughed for so long that Garrett saw Molly smile faintly.

"I'm sorry," the old man said finally, wiping at his eyes. "You should have seen your faces. Ol' Man Mississippi carried you off farther than you ever thought you'd go, didn't he? Did the same to me once."

A sudden rumble of thunder startled Garrett. The dog lifted its ears, cocking its head to one side. Garrett looked out the window in time to see a brilliant flash of blue-white lightning. A second later, thunder shook the house. Then the clouds opened, and the rain came down so hard that it was almost impossible to hear the old man when he spoke.

"You two better pull your raft up into the yard before you lose it downriver."

Garrett stood up and went to the door, Molly right behind him. As they stepped out into the downpour, lightning crackled overhead and struck somewhere so close that Garrett felt the ground tremble.

Chapter Twelve

Molly shrank from the cold deluge of rain, bending nearly double as she ran. Maybe the old man would let them stay here until the rain let up—maybe they could even sleep one night under his roof, or at least in his shed.

Garrett was a little ways ahead of her. The cloudburst continued, big drops of rain falling in nearly solid sheets. The ground streamed with little rivulets of water rushing downhill. Molly slid on the muddy path, bumping into Garrett from behind.

They waded in beside the raft, almost knee-deep in water. "It's come up nearly a foot since we got here," Garrett said, breathing hard.

Molly tried to remember how far out of the water

they had pulled the raft. It was nearly floating now, only two or three of the logs solidly on the island. "Let's drag it up the path," Molly said, leaning close so he could hear her over the rain.

"The path is too steep," Garrett shouted back. "Let's pull it around that way. I saw a place where we can get it all the way up into the yard, I think."

Molly glanced up. The sky was so dark with clouds that it felt like evening—even though she knew it was still midday. Lightning crackled to life overhead, turning the world into a flickering nightmare for a few seconds. The boom of thunder was quick and loud. The lightning was striking close by. Molly shivered.

"Take that side," Garrett was shouting.

She took hold of the rope. Garrett waded out, pulling the raft with him. Molly kept up, walking parallel to him, staying in the shallows.

"There!" Garrett shouted the word and pointed. Molly nodded. She could see the place he was talking about. Where the island curved away from them, the land rose more gradually—and there was almost no brush to block the way.

As they followed the skirt of the island, the slow current began to push the raft along. Molly waded in thigh-deep water—Garrett was in nearly to his waist. Molly found herself staring at the body of the dead snake, lying still now, in the middle of the raft.

Garrett suddenly slipped and went under. Molly froze for an instant, then he bobbed up, swimming a few strokes to catch hold of the side of the raft. He dragged himself onto it and faced her. "Just a little farther!" He was gesturing ahead.

Molly pulled hard. Without Garrett on the far side, the raft was clumsy and heavy. As she waded along, making slower progress, Garrett was securing their makeshift paddle and his pole. He reached out to lift the body of the snake. It was limp. "Should we keep it?"

Molly shook her head. The stew in her belly made it an easy decision. She thought about the warm little house as she pulled her feet free of the deep mud, step by step. She wished they could just go in out of the pouring rain and sleep until tomorrow. The raft snagged at the branches of a weeping willow that grew just at the high-water mark.

"Come deeper. Just a step or two," Garrett yelled over a roll of thunder.

Molly pushed the raft gently away from herself,

feeling the water deepen as she cleared the willow branches. The current caught the raft and floated it forward, around the end of the island.

"Just a little farther," Garrett shouted over the rain. "Can you do it alone?"

Molly nodded, slogging through water almost waist deep now. A massive rumble caught her attention, and she waited for the sky to flash blue-white veins of lightning. The rumble rose steadily.

"What's that?" Garrett shouted.

Molly looked up at him. He had twisted around, facing upriver. The rumble was louder than the rain now, and the sound was rising. Molly slipped and stumbled backward. She regained her balance and lurched forward, catching the edge of the raft. The strange sound was swelling, filling the air with an odd vibration that grated on Molly's ears.

"Oh my God!" Garrett yelled. "A levee broke somewhere above us."

A second later, in the murky false-dusk of the storm, Molly understood. She had time to whirl toward the island, then to turn back. She felt Garrett's hand close on her wrist. Then the raft was rising, spinning. Molly felt the current swirling around her legs, lifting her with the raft as the crest rose beneath them. Garrett dragged her forward onto the logs.

"Hang on!" he screamed.

Molly turned upriver, watching helplessly as a wall of dark water came toward them. One instant she was staring at it, the next it was shoving them forward, the logs bunching under the sudden force, pinching her fingers painfully. She cried out, then coughed when the dirty water closed over her head, filling her mouth.

She felt the rough bark slide against the palms of her hands as the water overpowered her, prying her from the raft. There was a pressure in her lungs, and her pulse pounded against her temples. Fighting the currents, Molly swam aimlessly, frantically trying to find the surface. Her legs scraped hard against something, and it felt as if her skin was being torn.

She opened her eyes, then closed them again, terrified by the darkness of the water. Wrenching around, swimming in another direction, Molly could feel the incredible strength of the current tumbling her over and over, like a boll of cotton in the wind. It was impossible to tell which way was up.

A stinging pain in her left hand made Molly double

up, her whole body curling into a crescent. The pain seemed to spread from her hand up her arm as the water churned, tumbling her over. When her head rose above the surface, it took Molly an instant to realize it. She pulled in a deep breath, then coughed.

Gasping and choking, she tilted her head back, keeping her face out of the water. The incredible roaring sound had faded, but she could still hear it. A stunningly bright flash of red made her aware that her eyes were closed, and she opened them in time to see the next bolt of lightning streak the sky.

The ache in her hand was receding. She managed to drag in another shuddering breath and began to tread water. Something nudged at her shoulder, and she spun around, her arms flailing, terrified it was another snake, hoping desperately that it was Garrett's helping hand.

It was neither. She looked past the curling root that had touched her to see a half-submerged tree trunk. It was enormous, an old magnolia, its April blooms half open.

Perched on a slender branch was a mockingbird. It canted its head to one side, its beadlike eyes fixed upon her as she struggled to pull herself up out of the water. When her clutching hands came within a few feet of it, it flew away.

Aching and coughing, Molly worked her way upward and collapsed on the broad trunk. After a time, she raised her head and looked around, hoping to see Garrett nearby. When she didn't, she sat up, careful of her balance. Turning upriver, then down, she felt a cold fear settling low in her stomach. She couldn't see the raft, or Garrett, or even the old cabin on its little island of high ground. A spatter of rain stung her face.

When the crest hit them, Garrett had tried hard to hold on to Molly. The water had been incredibly strong, yanking him backward, then forward again. The raft logs had bruised his ribs and scraped deep gouges on his belly. Somehow he had hung on.

Now, crouched on the raft, blinking as he tried to see through the rain, Garrett clenched his jaw to keep his teeth from chattering. Molly had been right with him. She had been next to him, and he had reached out to grab her wrist. How had this happened? How had the river taken her so far from him that he couldn't spot her at all?

"Molly! he shouted. His throat was tight, and his voice sounded rough. "Molly!" he tried to shout louder. There was no answer.

Garrett twisted around on the raft, looking in one direction, then another. Lightning brightened the sky, then winked out. In every direction he could see only the desolate brown water. What if she had drowned? The thought pushed its way into his mind, and he tried to argue with it. Of course she hadn't drowned. Molly swam better than he did. Unless she had hit her head on the raft or something else and . . .

Be still, he commanded his thoughts. Purposefully, he stood up and balanced carefully on the raft. All he could see were boards and branches—Molly's faded yellow dress was nowhere in sight. The rain shortened his vision, he knew. He shouted her name again. Then again. He shouted until his voice began to crack and weaken. Then he forced himself to calm down and take stock.

The surge had passed, and the water was moving slowly all around him now. He still had his pole. But Molly's bag was gone, he noticed. The water had somehow loosened the knots. She would be upset. Her mother couldn't easily spare a good kitchen knife. Garrett lifted his gaze to the water. The river was full of the wreckage it had caused. Garrett stared at a fan of long planks jutting up at a ridiculous angle. Whatever they were attached to had sunk. He untied the drawer front and paddled slowly toward them left-handed, his right hand too blistered to use much. When he was close enough, he could see the scalloped edge of a tin roof. The weight of the metal had pulled the wood beneath the surface. Garrett pushed the drawer front hard against the side of the planks, backing the raft away a few feet.

"Molly! Molly?" Garrett cleared his throat, then kept shouting. Where should he look? Where would the water have taken her? He felt muddled, as though he had awakened from a too-long sleep. The crest had taken everything familiar away and had replaced it with . . . this. He scanned the slow-moving water, looking eastward through the still-sprinkling rain.

"Molly!" This time his voice clattered off the planks, coming back to him an instant later. Not quite an echo, just a strange, splintered shout. He turned his head and called her name once more. This time, a bird burst out of the branches of a drowned tree. Garrett looked up to watch it fly, then sat down slowly, wondering why he hadn't noticed before. He was looking *up* at the trees again. The water was lower here.

Garrett scrambled to the center of the raft, laying the drawer front down and untying his pole. He started to turn back, then decided to anchor the drawer front to the raft. The crest had come without warning, and there were levees all along the river. Any one of them could break.

Trembling as the rain fell harder, Garrett gingerly pushed the pole into the water, careful of his blisters. When it hit bottom, he found himself fighting tears. He shook his head, forcing himself to stop. There was no reason to cry. He refused to believe that Molly was dead.

He began to pole the raft along, then stopped to tear a strip from his shirttail to pad his blistered right hand. He passed through the wreckage, making his way around an upside-down barn, then a thirty-foot length of picket fence.

Here, in the slower water, he could see more than boards and trees. He spotted a mass of red feathers, all moving in the current like slender leaves in a breeze. Going past, he saw the curved neck and sightless eyes of a drowned rooster.

A little farther on, poling around a fallen oak tree, the raft bumped into a drowned mule. Garrett shoved the raft backward and skirted the floating animal.

"Molly?" He barely whispered her name this time. Pulling in a huge breath and refusing to look backward at the mule, Garrett poled onward.

"Molly!" This time his voice worked. "Molly!" He managed a shout. "Molllyyy!" He roared her name at the rain, at the death-filled water, at the darkening sky. And this time, he heard an answer.

Chapter Thirteen

At first Molly had been able to do nothing besides cling to the tree trunk, her face pressed against the bark. Then she had shouted for Garrett, but he hadn't answered her. Every time lightning split the sky, she flinched, and the thunder seemed to shake her very soul. She could not see Garrett, or the raft.

The lightning got closer. The floodwater was lit like a flawed mirror with every crackling bolt. She squeezed her eyes shut against the image of the water's surface, cluttered with the floating remains of homes and lives. Was Mayersville gone now, too? Molly thought about her family and clenched her fists, sending a fierce, pleading prayer heavenward.

Then she rose up to her knees and tried shouting Garrett's name again.

The lightning gave her irregular glimpses of the water around her, but the rolling thunder swallowed her cries. Molly felt a shudder go through the tree trunk and she sat bolt upright, thinking for a moment that lightning had struck dangerously close. But there was no flash of light, nor smell of burnt wood.

She shifted her weight to her knees and rocked back on her heels. A second shudder went through the tree. She heard an odd groaning sound and scrambled forward to grab a broken branch that jutted up at an angle from the broad trunk. The branch seemed to move downward a few inches, and she readjusted her feet to keep her balance.

"It's turning," Molly whispered to herself. As if hearing her, the tree rolled a little farther to one side. Molly imagined the underwater half of the big old magnolia, its reaching branches spreading far enough to touch the muddy bottom—the water around it not quite deep enough to float it. Was the current strong enough to roll it like a wheel?

The next flash of lightning showed Molly a

swelling that connected three of the knuckles on her left hand. It looked grotesque, but she felt no pain as she shifted her grip to another branch.

The tree moved in little jerks, rolling over so far that Molly had to scramble sideways to keep from being carried into the water. On the upstream side, branches churned and rose, thrashing above her head like a leafy Ferris wheel.

Molly hung on instinctively as the branch she held on to lifted, then arced downward. She gasped in a deep breath the instant before she was plunged into the river. She let go of the branch, feeling leaves and twigs whip at her legs and back as she tried to swim clear of the rolling tree.

A glancing blow on her shoulder slowed Molly, but she swam desperately, struggling to reach the surface. All around her, the water roiled with slicing branches and leaves that stung her face and confused her.

Kicking frantically, fighting to get away from the tree, Molly didn't feel the odd tug at the back of her shift at first. Then, her collar tightened around her throat and she felt herself being pulled backward. The tree had caught hold of her, and it was dragging her deeper. Molly flailed at the water, twisting, wrenching around, then trying to reach behind herself with both hands.

Her fingertips brushed the bough that held her captive, but she couldn't get a grip on it. Panicked, kicking, she managed to hook one foot over a thick branch. She shoved hard and felt her collar begin to tear. Bracing both feet, she shoved herself backward and the cloth gave way. Desperate, lungs aching, she swam toward the surface.

Stark, silver veins of lightning lit the sky as Molly's face burst into the cool afternoon air. For a few seconds, she could only breathe. The air was sweet; it was delicious. Her thoughts spun giddily as she treaded water, turning to face the tree. As she watched, it rolled onward, churning the water to foam as it moved downstream.

Molly waited for another flash of lightning to search for something that could serve her as a float. Debris dotted the river, but none of it was close, and it was hard to tell boards from drowned trees or dead farm animals in the rain-grayed light.

Her arms beginning to ache, Molly turned a slow circle in the water. A line of standing treetops caught her eye. Not knowing what else to do, she swam toward them. The fourth tree had a limb level enough for her to rest upon. She hugged the trunk, shivering and miserable as the rain thickened into another downpour. Then, through the sound of the storm, she heard Garrett's voice. It was faint and distant and unmistakable. She struggled to her feet and shouted an answer.

"Molly!" Garrett shouted, whirling to face the sound of her voice and very nearly tipping the raft. Her answer was faint but distinct, and he began poling toward the sound of her voice.

"Garrett!" This time he could hear how desperate she sounded. He answered her, and she shouted back again. He felt a knot deep inside begin to loosen and he poled fast, no longer feeling the chill of the rain or the sharp stab of pain in his right hand every time he touched bottom and pushed forward.

The lightning was moving farther and farther away as the rain let up, taking the rumbling thunder with it. Garrett squinted upward. It had to be late in the day—maybe even early evening. Even though it had come only in flashes, the lightning had made it possible for him to see downriver a ways. Now that it was gone, he was aware of how he had been depending on it to pick his way through the debris in the water.

He followed the sound of Molly's voice, calling back to her every time she shouted. He bumped into a floating oil drum and had to slow to maneuver past it. When he looked up again, he realized that Molly's shouts were leading him toward a stand of drowned trees.

"Garrett? I'm in the gum tree—the big one—can you see me?"

His eyes followed the sound of her voice. He brought the raft around, poling steadily until he was directly beneath her. For a moment, they just stared at each other, grinning.

"You look like a drowned rat," she said.

"You look like a rat that drowned last week," he teased back.

Molly's smile dimmed and went out. "I've never been this scared."

"Me either," he admitted.

Molly climbed down, stepping shakily onto the raft as he steadied her. They both sat down quickly to keep the raft from tilting beneath them. He used his pole to push against the tree, turning downriver. "You rest awhile. I'll see how far I can get us before dark."

Molly sat on the raft, running her hand lightly over the wood, smiling as though she were delighted to see an old friend. "If you give out, I'll take a turn," she said.

Garrett nodded, an odd tightness in his throat. If they ever made it home, he was going to tell Willard and Earle that Molly Bride had more courage than they would ever have, put together. Times ten.

Chapter Fourteen

Night fell, and the cloud cover was so thick that the moon was hidden. Molly sat quietly, listening to the steady soft splash of Garrett's poling. She was weary, but she couldn't sleep.

"I lost the sack," Garrett told her. "And your mother's knife."

Molly shook her head. "Damnable river," she said, then blushed because she had cursed.

"Do you hear that?" Garrett asked suddenly. "A woman's voice?"

Molly started to shake her head, but then a ruddy sparkle off to the west caught her eye. A fire? Without saying anything more, Garrett shifted direction, poling toward it.

The voices became more distinct as they got closer. Soon, Molly could make out the group of people that were sitting around the fire. There were fifteen or twenty of them. She could see tents, or maybe just blankets, hung on a line at the edge of the firelight.

"Hello!" Garrett shouted as the raft glided close.

The people fell silent instantly, and Garrett called out again. Molly stared at the fire, imagining its warmth, as the people around it turned to stare in their direction.

The raft ran gently aground, and she stood up slowly, leaning on Garrett as they stepped off. The strip of dry ground was long and narrow, and she could see car tracks in the mud. One man, carrying a torch, led three or four other men toward them.

"It's what's left of their levee," she said quietly as they dragged the raft up out of the water. She heard Garrett make a sound of assent. She felt her nerves quieting. Just standing on solid ground made her less frightened.

"Who's out there?" a man's voice rang out.

"We're from upriver," Garrett called back, brushing at his muddy pants. "From Mayersville."

"We thought maybe you were the Red Cross folks," the man said, coming close enough that he didn't have to raise his voice. He lifted his torch high enough to light their faces. Behind him Molly heard another man talking.

"Go on back and tell Alice that it's just two children."

Molly heard footsteps leaving as the man with the torch was leaning toward them. "When'd you eat last?"

Molly saw Garrett smile. "Once today, but not the day before."

"Come on up to the fire, then, both of you. You can warm up some and eat supper." He gestured with the torch.

As she and Garrett approached, Molly scanned the faces of the men and women waiting for them. There were no white people at all. She felt herself relax a little more. Then, an older woman handed them tin plates of chicken and dumplings and settled them on overturned orange crates near the fire—and the rest of her wariness disappeared.

"Did you see any boats?" a tall woman asked Molly. "A man in a flatboat all loaded up with people told us yesterday that someone would be back to take us into Vicksburg."

"We haven't seen anyone," Molly told her, "except one old man living in a cabin that was on high enough ground to still be dry."

"And an airplane," Garrett added.

The woman frowned. "Well, I expect he'll come anytime now, and you children can just go with us."

Molly waited until the women were talking among themselves. Then she leaned close to whisper to Garrett, "Vicksburg!"

Garrett shrugged. "We've talked about it dozens of times, but I never thought it'd come like this," he said quietly. "We ought to be able to find someone there who will take us upriver."

Molly nodded. It made sense. She sat silently, happy to be off the water. Slowly, the fire warmed her, drying her dress. The hot food was unbelievably delicious, and the conversation swirled around her.

"We saw two or three planes yesterday," the tall woman was saying. "But they sure didn't seem to see us."

"All the way down from Mayersville on that little

raft?" the older woman asked as she ladled up more dumplings.

Molly listened to Garrett as he answered politely. It was suddenly very hard for her to stop yawning. She tried not to be rude. The truth was, as soon as she had finished eating, the warmth of the fire made her drowsy. By the time the older woman led them to pallets of blankets crowded into a canvas-and-plank lean-to, Molly could only mumble a thank-you and lie down.

"Boat! I hear the boat!"

The shout woke Garrett with a start. For a few seconds, he was confused, then he looked out of the lean-to at the world of brown water and remembered where he was.

He untangled himself from the blankets and stood up. The men were already down by the water's edge. Molly was with four or five women, hurrying toward the men. For the first time, he saw there were two horses at the far end of the levee, grazing on the short grass that grew at the water's edge.

The day had dawned cloudy; the sky was the color of lead. Looking out across the flooded land,

Garrett could see a few other high points, and he wondered if people and animals were stranded on every one of them.

Garrett could hear the boat motor clearly now, and after a minute he spotted it, chugging out from behind a copse of trees. Garrett went to stand with everyone else near the water. The boatman cut the motor and tipped it forward as the skiff glided in. "How many are here?" he demanded.

The man who had carried the torch stepped forward. "Eleven of us." Then he pointed at Garrett and at Molly. "These two are from up Mayersville way. Came all the way on that little ol' raft, and they—"

"Load up now," the boatman interrupted. "I'll get you all down to Vicksburg."

Garrett cleared his throat. "We want to go back upriver, Mister," he said politely. "Molly and me, I mean. You think we can find someone to take us?"

The boatman's eyes raked him up and down, then he spat into the water. "Your best bet is in Vicksburg, son. Half of Mississippi is in the refugee camps there." He spat again, looking around at the little section of levee. "You'll find a northbound boat easier from there than from here, I expect."

Garrett glanced at Molly. She had moved aside. The women were trailing up and down the path, bringing their few belongings to load into the boat. The boatman looked bored, staring out over the water.

Garrett worked his way through the little knot of people and went to stand beside Molly. "I hate to leave the raft," Garrett said.

Molly nodded. "We'll build another one."

"You two about ready?" the boatman asked abruptly.

Garrett turned to see that the skiff had been pushed back into the water. The women were already sitting in it. The men were taking turns getting aboard. Molly went to share a bench with the tall woman. Garrett waited his turn, then got on and stood near the boatman. "We met an old man still in his cabin," Garrett told him. "On a little patch of high ground west of here, and north, I guess. It was upstream."

The boatman nodded brusquely. "I'll keep an eye out and pass the word."

As the motor sputtered to life, Garrett turned backward, staring at the raft as they moved out into the sluggish water. He saw Molly looking back, too. He kept the raft in sight as long as he could, then faced front.

The women kept up a conversation to pass the time, but Molly found she had little to say. The brown water slid beneath the boat, and the droning of the motor grated at her ears. Finally, the boatman turned. "This is Vicksburg, folks. I'm going to let you off up here on the levee above the graveyard," he shouted.

Molly followed his gesture. The levee was lined with boats of all sizes. There were oil and cargo barges, too, and the tugboats that had pushed them here. People stood shoulder to shoulder on them— there were no benches or seats. Someone had strung a low chicken-wire fence—probably, Molly thought, to keep people from falling off.

Molly let Garrett lead the way as they jumped from the boat to the levee, then turned back. "Mister? There's an old man and a dog stranded out—"

"The boy told me, Miss," the boat man interrupted her. She nodded and hurried to catch up with Garrett.

The crowds made her nervous. There were

hundreds of people milling around. Families stood in loose groups beside stacks of trunks and quilts. One woman had a rooster in a wire crate, and an old man was cradling a Victrola like a child. Most people didn't have much except what they were wearing. One little boy was coughing so hard that Molly couldn't bear to watch.

She scanned the dizzying mosaic of faces. White-aproned women made their way through the throng. Some of them wore white scarves with red crosses printed on the cloth. Molly stumbled on the muddy ground, accidentally shoving a man in front of her. He turned, scowling.

"I am so sorry," Molly said quickly.

He nodded brusquely. Molly stared after him as he walked away, wishing her father were there to take care of her.

"You all right?" Garrett asked, startling her.

She spun around to look into his eyes. "Yes. No. I just want to go home." She looked at the milling mass of people. There were a dozen babies wailing all at once. A man with a bloody bandage around his head was arguing with two other men.

"Let's go ask how we can get back upriver,"

Garrett said. Leading off, he stepped around two men carrying a stretcher. Molly glanced down as she passed, wincing when she saw an elderly woman, a little trickle of blood at the side of her mouth. Her eyes were open, but Molly was pretty sure she was dead.

"This way!" Garrett said over his shoulder, and Molly ran a few steps to catch up. She could see some kind of line forming in front of two white-aproned women. People were dragging their feet, shuffling along. Everyone looked weary.

Molly nearly ran into Garrett as a big man with a blond mustache blocked their path, his arms spread out like he was shooing chickens. "Have you registered yet?" he asked Garrett. "Are you alone, boy?"

"Registered?" Molly heard Garrett ask.

The man adjusted his hat. "Registered. A tag, do you have a tag? You're not from Vicksburg, are you? We don't allow the local children to come up to the camps, you know."

Garrett shook his head. "We're from Mayersville."

"We? Where's your family, son?" the big man asked, looking from Garrett to Molly, then back. "You need to get ahold of your folks. And your friend

here should go on up and get her tag. Were her par-
ents on that last barge?"

"No, sir," Garrett answered.

Molly shook her head when the man shifted his
gaze to her face. "My folks are back home," she said
quietly.

"Both of you need to get registered," the man
said, his voice loud, even over the noise of the
crowd. "Negroes over there." He pointed, his eyes
on Molly. Then he turned to Garrett. "Son, you can
come with me."

Molly looked at the mud beneath her feet. Of
course. The refugee camps would be segregated. She
just hadn't thought about it.

"Thank-you, sir," Garrett was saying clearly, looking up into the man's face. "We sure do thank you
for the advice." Garrett stood stiffly, his shoulders
squared, his chin jutted out.

Molly felt sick, like the world was shifting
beneath her feet. The white man said something else
to Garrett and clapped him on the back. Then he
strode off. Molly swallowed, her heart beating fast.
She didn't want to be alone, surrounded by so many
people and all of them strangers.

Garrett tilted his head, gesturing for her to follow. He walked along the edge of the levee to avoid the worst of the crowds. Across an expanse of brown water, Molly could see the town of Vicksburg rising up on hills that looked huge. She could see cars in the streets.

Garrett stopped, and she almost stepped on his heels. "You don't want to go to the camp, do you?"

She shook her head instantly. "No. My folks won't come here. My pa said he wasn't leaving the farm for anything."

Garrett nodded. "My mama's aunt Julia Pearl teaches school up in Yazoo County. Mama was talking about going there if the water got too high."

Garrett rubbed one hand across his face. "All right. You wait here, and I'll see if I can get someone to take us back upriver."

Molly watched him walk away. A little sprinkle of rain started up, cold against her face. She shivered, hugging herself. Garrett approached a man in a blue uniform jacket. The man gestured and shook his head. Then he pointed, and Molly saw Garrett nod and walk on up the levee. A moment later, he disappeared into the crowd.

KATHLEEN DUEY and KAREN A. BALE

Molly shivered again. It was raining harder, and it was all she could do to stand the milling and noise of the people around her. By the time Garrett finally came trotting back out of the crowd, she was biting at her lower lip.

As he got closer, she could see he was smiling. "There's a supply boat going up to Mayersville in about an hour. All we have to do is wait."

Molly started crying. She couldn't help herself. Now, if their families were safe, everything was going to be all right.

Chapter Fifteen

Lying on the deck, up against the pilot's house, Garrett kept dozing fitfully as the day wore on. The throbbing of the engine was numbing, and the brown water and submerged trees seemed to go on forever. Twice they passed boats headed downriver. Garrett saw one barge at a distance too, the tugboat painted red and white. All along the way they passed people who had pitched tents on the levee tops—often the only dry ground for miles.

The boat's captain had given them sandwiches and coffee, and for a few hours Garrett had felt better. Then, he had gotten sleepier than he'd ever been in his life.

Molly had finally curled up on a pile of bean sacks

beneath the shelter of a tarp that had been rigged over the deck. She didn't awaken when they stopped at Brunswick or at Weigant—or even when the pilot leaned out and shouted his occasional comments about the countryside they were passing.

"That's Steel Bayou off east, there. My granddaddy ran gunboats in and out of there back in sixty-four and sixty-five."

Garrett nodded to show he had understood, and the pilot went back to his constant scanning of the river's surface. When they passed the roof of the Homochitto cotton shed, Garrett stood. Uneasy, he walked around what remained of the piles of provisions, stretching, staring upriver. When he finally spotted the Mayersville levee, he woke Molly.

"What?" she murmured, then abruptly sat up, blinking. "Are we home?"

He nodded. "Pretty close. Look."

Together they stood looking at the flooded countryside. Garrett clenched his jaw when he spotted the roofline of his house. Only the peak was showing. The little barn he had freed of tye vine was completely submerged. "Lord," he whispered, feeling a shakiness that began in his heart and worked itself outward.

The boat pilot was slowing now, preparing to sidle in close to the levee. Molly was silent as they chugged past her place. Only the tops of the eaves were above the dark water. Chickens sat in a forlorn row along the edge of the roof. There was no other sign of life. Garrett tried to think of something to say—but he couldn't.

Garrett heard a shout and turned to look. Mr. Talbot, Bubba Lawlor, and one of the Bagley brothers had brought their skiffs up onto the slope of the levee. They stood waving their arms at the pilot. Silent, Molly stood close to Garrett as the throbbing engine brought them closer.

"Garrett Wood, is that you?" Mr. Talbot shouted. "Your mama is surely going to be glad to know you're alive."

Garrett leaned over the rail as the pilot cut the engine. "Do you know where she is? Are my sisters all right?"

Mr. Talbot had climbed up onto the levee road. He was nodding emphatically. "All fine, all fine, when I saw them last, except for the soaking we've all gotten these past few days. Your mama wanted to go on up to Yazoo City, but she stayed back hoping to find you. I took her out to the Indian mound south of town. Is that Joseph Bride's little gal I see behind you there?"

Garrett stepped aside as Molly came forward. "Mr. Talbot, are my folks still around here?" she called, her voice strained.

"We'll find them somewhere, I'm sure," he answered briskly as the pilot threw Bubba Lawlor a rope. "We got to get these groceries out to folks before dark if we can."

"I couldn't hardly come up against that current any faster than I did," the pilot said, jumping to the ground, then helping Molly and Garrett onto the levee road.

Garrett saw the worry on Molly's face and he tried to catch her eye, but the men had begun unloading supplies, and Mr. Talbot motioned for them to help.

Garrett and Molly carried tins of condensed milk and bags of sugar and wheat flour down the steep slope of the levee. The men divided up the goods among the boats, settling who would carry supplies where. Garrett kept remembering how the awful brown water had been lapping at the roof eaves. His cot was under it, and so was his mother's old bed, which had come from her mother. Everything. His little garden with its half-grown cabbage. He stiffened, realizing that the field where his father had died was now under the ugly, cold water, too. He glanced at Molly. Her face was ashen with worry.

Molly waited, staring anxiously out across the floodwater as the men dickered over the supplies. The jailhouse stood up out of the flood, but all the one-story buildings in town were either beneath the water or showing just their roof peaks. The road that led out of town was invisible now, only the crowns of a few trees marking the fence lines of the farms.

"Let's go, then," Mr. Talbot said. He and Garrett pushed the skiff downhill into the water that stood against the levee. He started his engine and motioned her and Garrett to sit on the forward bench.

Molly stared straight ahead, even when Garrett nudged her and pointed at the line of trees that marked the bayou. Mr. Talbot followed the levee closely to stay out of the tangle of tree limbs and floating junk. When they passed the lightning tree,

Garrett nudged her again and she saw him smile. Their tree was still leaning solidly on the hackberry a few feet above the water. Their money jar was safe in its knothole, at least for now. Molly smiled back at Garrett, then held herself rigid as they rounded the last of the trees and she could see her house.

The roofline was empty—she had seen that much going past on the boat. But now it became painfully obvious that no one could still be here. The whole barnyard was deep underwater. She couldn't see the cowshed, the chicken coop, or the rail fence of the mule pen.

"Nobody home," Mr. Talbot shouted over the clatter of the engine. "But I expect they got out all right. Most did. We'll find news of them soon enough."

Molly stared at his back as he guided the boat across their lower cornfield, then took a crooked path up along the edge of the woods. The road leading into Garrett's place made a good canal through the thickest part of the forest. They followed it eastward up to the old plantation road, then turned south again.

Molly began praying for her family's safety. People appeared as they heard the boat coming, and Molly strained to see anyone she knew, but couldn't make out faces in the dusky afternoon light.

Mr. Talbot maneuvered the skiff through a stand of oak trees. Then he cut the motor and ran it gently aground. Molly heard Garrett whoop and saw Mae and Ivy running toward him as he jumped out of the skiff. His mother and Ginny were close behind.

Molly almost stumbled getting out, her legs trembly. She stood off to one side, watching Garrett as his family surrounded him, all of them laughing and happy.

"I do believe there's someone who would like to talk with you," Mr. Talbot said from behind her. She turned, startled. A little ways off, coming at a run, she saw her father. She whirled and ran toward him. He caught her up in his arms and spun her in a circle. "Are the boys and Hope all right? And Ma?"

"No thanks to your fool of a father, they are all alive and well," he interrupted her gently. "I was wrong to try to stay as long as we did. Your ma may forgive me if I bring you back to her in one piece."

"Molly!" Garrett was breaking away from his tearful mother. He stood awkwardly for a second, then walked closer. Molly felt tears welling up in her eyes. Her father tugged at her hand, but she hesitated a second longer. "Thank you, Garrett Wood. For being my friend."

He grinned and hugged her, hard. "I'm the one who should thank you. See you in the morning?"

She nodded. "Meet you here."

Molly turned back to her father and smiled up at him. Then, she glanced at Garrett walking away. His sisters were dancing around him, pulling him along. Whatever else the flood did to her, it had proven one thing: Garrett Wood was her best and truest friend.

Turn the page for more
Survival stories in:

SURVIVORS

DEATH VALLEY:
CALIFORNIA, 1849

a novel by

KATHLEEN DUEY and KAREN A. BALE

Will was tired. He glanced at his father. How much farther were they going to walk? There was no game here. There hadn't been so much as a rabbit for three days. He shouldered his rifle. "Why don't we just go back to camp, Pa?"

His father turned, tugging his hat brim lower. "Your mother and sister can't go much longer without meat. Nor Eli, nor Jeb."

"Van Patten's brindled ox is about to die, anyway, Pa. Jess told me they're saying they'll still share—"

"I don't like depending on anyone's charity, Will."

Will pressed his lips together to keep from saying what was on his mind. If they had stayed in Illinois, if his father's dreams of California gold hadn't interfered with his good judgment, they would all be sitting around the hearth, stringing popcorn for the Christmas tree. Outside the windows would be snow on the ground, solid and white.

"Over there, Will."

Will followed his father's gesture. There were sparse clumps of sage growing from the rocky soil. As he stared, Will thought he saw the leaves vibrate. Something was crouched between the stalks, hiding. Will felt his mouth water, imagining rabbit stew.

"I'll get around to the side, Will. I'll flush it out toward you."

Will nodded without looking away from the wind-beaten sage. His father's boots ground against the rocky soil. There was no way to move silently here. The howling winter winds had scoured the topsoil, exposing a layer of gravel.

"Watch carefully," Will's father said quietly. "If it makes a run back this way, call out. Maybe I can get a shot at it."

Will glanced up, then his eyes returned to the sage. His father walked closer, as intent as any mountain lion, knees bent, his rifle half raised. Will said a little prayer and raised his own rifle. They had almost used up the bags of flour and rice they'd bought from the Mormon storekeep in the new little settlement on Salt Lake.

Will held the rifle steady, breathing evenly, waiting. Without meaning to, he pictured their old kitchen table, the one they'd left beside the trail a few weeks out of Fort Laramie the first time they had had to lighten the wagon. It felt like their lives were scattered behind them all the way back to Illinois. Most of their furniture was gone; they had traded his mother's trunk for new iron tires on the wagon wheels.

Will glanced at his father—he was slowly advancing on the clump of sage. Will allowed himself to think about what a real supper would be like. He could see it so clearly, smell the inviting scents of his mother's chicken and dumplings, her fruit pies, steamed sweet corn and yams. His mouth flooded with saliva again.

"Will!"

He jerked his head up to look at his father.

"Is it still in there? Did you see it run?"

Will shook his head, pretty sure he hadn't actually closed his eyes. He was so tired. They hadn't had enough water for days—or enough food, really, even though the families were sharing meat whenever anyone had to kill one of the oxen.

The sage shook suddenly, and Will pulled the hammer all the way back, waiting tensely. Then he settled the rifle snug into his shoulder and aimed at the blur of motion that burst clear a second later. Steady, deliberate, he pulled the trigger.

"You got him! He's a big one," Will's father called, holding the rabbit up by one hind leg.

Will smiled, tapping powder into his rifle. He rammed the shot home, then slid the rod back into its scabbard, reaching for the pouch that held his percussion caps.

Following his father's impatient gesture, he began to wade through the scrubby line of sage where the rabbit had hidden. There was a sudden scrabbling sound, and two more rabbits burst out of the brush. Lifting the rifle, he killed the first rabbit. The second ran on as he stopped to reload.

"I'll get it," Pa yelled, and broke into a run. Will heard the shot and his father's jubilant shout. He smiled. So there would be three rabbits for supper.

Ma wouldn't have to ladle carefully to make sure there was a fair share of the meat in everyone's broth. Tonight, there would be plenty.

"We'll gut and skin these here, son," Pa called.

Will started toward him. All the men had taken to cleaning their game outside camp. It saved the families with less food the torture of watching a long supper preparation. The Hogans were the worst off. Will hated bringing meat into camp, walking past their wagon. They had seven children, and Mr. Hogan was a terrible shot. Back home, he had been a fine farmer, always helping his neighbors in bad years. All the Van Pattens still gave him meat because of that. Otherwise, his children would have starved by now.

For the last month there had been little game to share. Mr. Bailey kept all his meat for himself. Mr. Tolford still gave away some, mostly to the Hogans, but he jerked more meat now and kept it back for himself and Moses, his hired man. They were both good shots. Mr. Tolford's wagons were full of supplies, not bedding and furniture. He had even brought oats for his mule team.

"Gather up some sage, Will." Pa leaned his rifle

against a flat rock the size of a bedstead, then pulled his slender skinning knife from its scabbard.

"Yes, sir." Will propped his rifle beside his father's and laid the rabbits on the rock. Then he headed toward the brush.

The sage stems were hollow and dry and snapped easily. The sharp, clean smell of the leaves tickled at Will's nostrils. When he started back, his father was just finishing the first rabbit. Will spread the sage out so his father could lay the carcass down, pink and glistening, then set the skin to one side. Will broke off a handful of leaves and rubbed them over the still warm meat. It was early, but flies would gather soon.

"Your mother will be glad to see these," Will's father said as he gutted the second rabbit, then made the long, quick cuts that freed the skin.

A faint rustling caught Will's attention. He half-turned, one hand full of sage leaves. Twenty paces away, among the dense papery leaves of a buckwheat bush, he saw a slight movement. Suddenly, a big jackrabbit, twice the size of the cottontails they had killed, rushed into the open.

Whirling, leaning to reach across the rock for his rifle, Will had a split-second daydream of a dramatic, last-second shot, of being the one to bring home enough meat to last into tomorrow. Then he stepped on a rock that rolled beneath his foot. He struggled to keep his balance as he lurched sideways, falling into his father. As he hit the ground he heard his father cry out.

Will scrambled to his feet. His father's face had gone pale, and the knife lay at the base of the rock. There was a slanting gash across his father's thigh.

"What the—? Will, what are you doing?" Pa bent to press his hand over the wound.

Will stood still, shocked by the stream of blood pouring from between his father's fingers. "I was just—I saw a jackrabbit and I was just—"

"Tear some strips from your shirt, Will. Two or three, wide enough to cover this."

Will stared at his father for a second, still stunned by the ivory pallor in his face, the sheen of sweat on his skin.

"Do as I say, Will!"

Will fumbled at his shirttail, his hands shaking. It

had all happened so fast. He shrugged his shirt off, then gripped the cloth, hesitating an instant. His entire life it had been drilled into him to take care of the clothing that had cost his mother so many hours to sew. And she sewed well. The hem was sturdy, the stitches so close together that for an eternal moment Will could not manage to start a tear. Clumsy, frantic, glancing involuntarily at the blood soaking his father's trousers, Will managed to rip a long strip of cloth and extended it toward his father.

"I can't. You'll have to do it, Will." Pa's voice sounded distant, faint. He worked at his suspenders buttons and slid his trousers down. The cut was even deeper than Will had thought. Frightened, Will tore two more bandage strips. He forced himself to concentrate, to push the edges of the gash together, to bind his father's leg tightly. The blood soaked the bandages almost instantly, but once they were tied off, it slowed to a trickle. Pa pulled his trousers up and fastened his suspenders again.

"Finish skinning that last rabbit, son."

Will looked up at the calmness in his father's voice. "I'm sorry, Pa. I'm really sorry. I just thought—"

"We don't have time for that now, Will. Finish the last one, and let's get going."

"Can you walk, Pa?"

His father laughed, an ugly grating sound. "Unless you're going to carry me."